The Mountains Hold Both Light and Darkness

Private Investigator Helen Hartsock seeks out
Martha Phelps: a woman with a mysterious past and
fiercely loyal friends.
And deep knowledge of secrets the mountains hold.

A lonely old man. A disturbed young man.
A past filled with grief.
Will Larry and Joan solve the puzzles they face?

More than the usual number of unusual people call
Maple Ridge home.
But Carol and Sid never expect what they discover
on a snowy December night.

A young trainee. An old mentor. A puzzling death.
Join Mo and Doc Em as they face the most prolific
killer of all.

Regina Burke races to keep her sweet Trevor from
driving into a nightmare neither imagined.
Will she find him in time, before the nightmare wins?

John returns home for the reunion of his dreams.
Pete faces his family history, however unwillingly.
How will one woman's reckoning shape their future?

The Garbage Belt

Plurapod Pathogen

The Changes Cascade

Near Future Forward (with Jason A. Adams)

Dispatches from the Galaxy: A Space Opera Novella Trio

Dangerous Days on a Pleasure Planet

Storms of Future Past:

Dreaming the Storm

Joining the Storm

Into the Storm

Fighting the Storm

Storms of the Heart

Storms of Future Past Omnibus

Voices Through Time:

Songs in the Mountain

Secrets in the Land

Sorrows in the Earth

Walking the Ghosts

The Odd Society:

Independent by Means of Magic

Protected by Means of Magic

Collections:

Anthologies *with Jason A. Adams*:

JASON A. ADAMS
KARI KILGORE

SHADOWS MOUNTAIN DEEP

Spiral Publishing, Ltd.

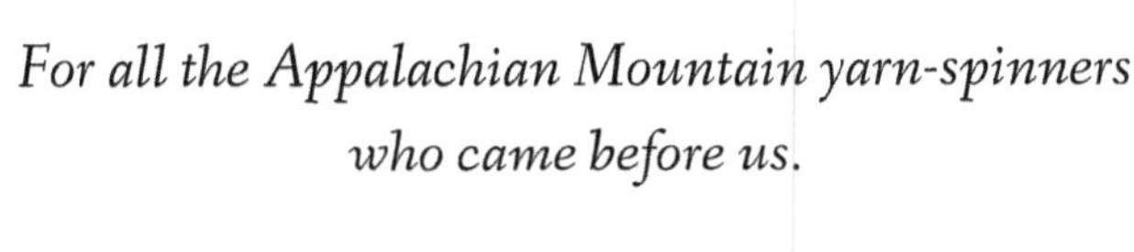

*For all the Appalachian Mountain yarn-spinners
who came before us.*

CONTENTS

GREETINGS FROM THE SHADOWS

KARI KILGORE AND JASON A. ADAMS

Kari:

Mystery or crime fiction has always seemed like a natural fit in our native Appalachian Mountains.

The most obvious reason, especially to folks not from around here, is probably the impression that we're almost like another country. Our language and dialects are similar to what many think of as generally Southern. But there's a rhythm and music to the words that's uniquely part of these mountains.

For example, the name of our mountains and our region is pronounced app-a-LATCH-ian here in Virginia, like a door latch. We definitely appreciate folks who make the effort to get it right.

I grew up mostly in Southern Illinois—another region with a richly diverse culture and frequently mispronounced place names. Not quite St. Louis, not quite Chicago. Call it farm country with an urban awareness. So I don't speak with the same soft mountain accent I grew up hearing from my parents, grandparents, cousins, and various kinfolk.

The specific turns of phrase are easy to call to mind, though, and they seem to naturally flow through my fingers when I write with characters from here. My husband Jason A. Adams had a similarly removed upbringing as the child of an Air Force pilot. Both of his parents were also natives of our coalfield region in far Southwestern Virginia, so he grew up spending time here much like I did.

No matter where we find ourselves, these mountains are home.

We share many of the same memories and attitudes despite growing up in such different areas and cultures, and he can also conjure our musical native dialect in his stories.

I'll freely admit he does a much better job reading that accent out loud than I do.

Another aspect of our mountains that lends itself to mystery is the landscape itself. We don't have the towering peaks of the Rockies out west, partly because our mountains are so much older. The erosion and weathering over all those eons created our close, narrow valleys, with thick forests all around.

Add a sparse population and the tendency for fog and mist, and people understandably wonder what kinds of secrets are hidden away along our shadowy creeks and hollers (the proper local pronunciation for hollow. I happen to be sitting in one as I type this).

We also have a well-deserved reputation for being a bit distrustful of outsiders. This one isn't only cultural, even for a group of people who do value our privacy and independence. Unfortunately, there's also a long history of folks from other places deciding to show up and claim our natural resources of timber and coal, then send the profits elsewhere and leave the damaged land behind.

The same thing happens all too often in the modern era as well, with numerous factories or high-tech call centers getting built, providing good job opportunities for a time, then left abandoned, along with the workers, families, and communities who depended on those jobs.

Yet another twist of the unusual that I love about our region is the incredible diversity of people who settled here over time. The Scots-Irish influence is undeniable, certainly coming from someone with a family name like Kilgore. But a quick look into our history reveals people arriving from not only all over Britain, but from all over Europe, with a significant population from Hungary and Italy, and from the

Middle East to go along with a healthy African-American influx.

My own genetic testing confirmed that while I do indeed have Scottish and German ancestry, my forbearers also came from all over Europe, Western Africa, and Egypt.

I and many other Appalachians are the very definition of a melting pot. Our culture and politics and music and art are every bit as diverse as our landscapes and our DNA.

We're also generally well-educated, intelligent, curious, welcoming of visitors who aren't trying to exploit us, and excited about moving forward into the future, while maintaining a deep sense of pride about where we come from.

Now bring all of that together with our tendency to enjoy storytelling, and it's no wonder I often write stories set close to home. Inspiration is all around me every day, and my memories overflow with fascinating characters, settings, and odd goings on.

And many of those yarns end up leaning toward mystery and crime fiction of all subgenres.

My first story in *Shadows Mountain Deep* leans into the distrust of outsiders for certain, and the common scenario of someone moving away for work, or growing up elsewhere like I did. *The Definition of Crime* brings the dislocation of a character returning from the big city—with an insider/outsider perspective—square into the middle of an especially protective group in an already tight-knit mountain town.

The beautiful and challenging geography of our mountains takes center stage in *A Race Against Tea Time*. So many aspects of modern technology that people take for granted in cities or more forgiving terrain are less reliable along our curvy roads and deep valleys. This story brings our community spirit and fierce determination to look out for each other into play as well.

The charming town of Bountyfield is a great example of one of my favorite parts of writing. I've created my own network of fictional towns all across the region over the years, and I had a great time playing with that shared geography in *A Race Against Tea Time*. You'll encounter towns from several of my series in one suspenseful tale. To learn more and visit the other thriving towns inside my head, including Bountyfield's *Voices Through Time* series, check out www.KariKilgore.com/TalesFrom-Appalachia.

My final entry in this collection fits into another series, and it switches gears to cozy mystery and the winter holidays. *Adventures in Winter Driving* visits Maple Ridge (which you'll recognize from *A Race Against Tea Time*), an important setting in my apocalyptic series *Storms of Future Past*. This prequel story introduces two characters in their youth and shows Maple Ridge in happier times.

That's not to say all is calm and normal by any means. Not when visiting the secluded home of the town's most eccentric and secretive resident.

One of the best parts about putting collections like this together with Jason is seeing how our writing worlds overlap, much like our family backgrounds do. You'll catch a glimpse of one of his series settings, which I'm more than happy to borrow from time to time for my own fiction. But I'll let him tell you more about that.

I hope we write a few proper crossover stories sometime in the future, and bring our imaginary worlds together, much like we've done in real life.

I hope you enjoy reading these stories as much as I enjoyed writing them. Check out all kinds of mysterious tales at www.KariKilgore.com/Mystery.

You can also visit www.KariKilgore.com to learn more about me and find other short stories, along with novellas, novels, and more collections.

If you want to keep up with what I'm doing next, get free stories and access to exclusive ebooks and print versions not available anywhere else, find out about Kickstarters and other fun projects, and see adorable pet photos, head over to www.Confidential AdventureClub.com. Hope to see you there!

And last but certainly not least, thank you for your support of me and my writing. It means the world to me and keeps me coming back to tell the next tale.

Jason:

"Y'all ain't from around here, are ya?"

A simple question that can mean friendly curiosity or angry suspicion, depending on a whole slew of circumstances.

The Appalachian Mountains in general—and the deep hollers and long, tall ridges in particular—are a fascinating blend of misty forests, fiercely independent folks who can be as welcoming as they can ferocious, and a tangled pile of superstitions, folklore, and tall tales both ancient and new.

My ancestors landed in the pointy end of Virginia for the same reason a lot of other settlers did. Land was cheap, game was plentiful, and the tax man was absent. Freedom to be who they were without any fuss and bother, in other words.

And that freedom, as it so often does, sometimes means the freedom to do less than noble things upon our fellow humans. If you don't believe me, get on your favorite music-acquisition source and look up "murder ballads."

What's interesting to me is that the Appalachians don't hold any more criminals than any other group of people. It's that storytelling part of our nature that takes over.

A family squabble that led to a dozen dead (bad enough) expanded into a famous legend of all-out mountain warfare. Stories abound of Civil War gold buried long ago and forgotten. Bootleggers still outfoxin' the lawman (though the products have changed). Families with dark secrets protected by even darker means.

This collection of stories by Kari Kilgore and me explores some of those story seeds. I'll let Kari tell you about hers, and I'll tell you about mine. That's another thing, we don't want someone else tellin' our bidness. Even, and often especially, when it comes to members of our own families.

In *Discovering the Obvious*, Sheriff Larry Crabtree, one of my favorite characters to write, manages to unearth something no one is trying all that hard to hide.

The Number One Killer is another story about death, and about that good, patient mentorship we all need when we're starting out.

Finally, *Reunion and Redemption* is about coming home, finding your past, and reconciling it with your present. It's also about the hope of a better future, and that's a fine hope indeed.

I truly hope you have as much fun reading these stories as I did writing them. Because let's face it. Dead bodies or not, crime stories are *fun*. They may be dark and twisted, or the solver of the crime may be a sweet granny with a nose for gossip. But they're all fun, both to read and to write.

If you like what you read and want more of my Appalachian stories, Sheriff Larry mysteries, or any of the other nuts that occasionally drop from the Brain Squirrels in my mental garden, be sure to head over to www.JasonAdamsBooks.com and sign up for my newsletter, or just to leave a note to let me know what's on your mind.

SHADOWS MOUNTAIN DEEP

KARI KILGORE

AUTHOR OF WICKED BONE AND SONGS IN THE MOUNTAIN

THE DEFINITION OF CRIME

*For everyone who knows the secrets
and knows how and when to share them*

THE DEFINITION OF CRIME

When it came to laundromats, Helen Hartsock had definitely seen worse in her years as a private investigator.

Much, much worse.

The Laurel Gap Lost Sock Laundry had been recently remodeled, and quite nicely. All the smaller washers and dryers were gleaming white, all the industrial-sized monsters bright polished steel. No dents or rust spots in sight.

The row of chairs up against the spotless plate glass window up front was made up of the same shiny plastic curved variety Helen remembered from the 70s and 80s. Even had the two strange little holes low on the back that never quite made sense. But rather than puke green or depressing hospital tan, these chairs were cheery pink and bright yellow.

Same with the long waist-high tables that ran down the middle of the space. Alternating pink or yellow, they were finished around the edges with honest-to-goodness chrome. Like a Formica factory had closed down and sold all the remainders to a laundromat factory.

The neatly swept floor looked like it had the same rock-hard speckly white tile from thirty years ago, but no signs of cracks or grime around the grout.

Of course the cleanest, most cared-for space dedicated to laundry in the world was going to have that *smell*. Harsh detergent, overlaid with too many varieties of cloying floral fabric softener, liberally seasoned with hot dryer lint. Not Helen's favorite, but miles better than some of the mildew and stagnant water reeking places she'd been forced to spend time in on one assignment or another.

Not too crowded early on a Wednesday evening, either. Helen had the place almost to herself, with only two of the washers and one dryer occupied at the moment. The middle-aged man tending to all those clothes sat in another cluster of plastic chairs toward the back, hunched over a laptop and lost to the world. Late March in the mountains seemed a bit chilly out for his faded Atlanta Braves t-shirt and even more faded denim shorts.

She thought he might be muttering to himself,

but the low roar of the dryer and irregular ticking of something in the washers drowned him out.

Helen had spent too many years watching people, predicting them, understanding them, to not recognize laundry day attitude and attire when she saw it.

Other than him, she had her pick of machines, tables, and the huge rolling baskets with metal clothes bars across the top. The baskets were as clean and new as everything else. And yes, that same optimistic yellow and pink.

She dumped her usual road-trip wardrobe into a washer closer to the front. Three pairs of jeans, two of non-descript brown khakis, muted button-up shirts and t-shirts. A whole lot like what she had on. Couple of nightshirts, bundles of socks and underthings, and even those were...not colorful.

Boring, yes. Easy to wash when travel made that a necessity, you bet. Sturdy enough to stand up to shredding washers and overly hot dryers nowhere near as nice as The Lost Sock Laundry, of course.

Ordinary enough to blend in with the locals? Absolutely.

Since she'd been coming in at this exact time—between shift changes at the coal mine and after the after-school and dinnertime rush—no one noticed this was her third time washing everything this week.

Partly because she got here right before the usual crowd of regulars wandered in.

Helen was betting on one of those regulars keeping to her schedule like she had for the past week. Seemed plenty likely, since Laurel Gap hardly provided a dizzying array of nighttime entertainment options.

Memories of Helen's own childhood and very young adulthood in another Appalachian mountain town not all that far away mainly consisted of riding around in cars, drinking, and getting high. Not what anyone would expect of a grown woman several years older than Helen was at forty-eight.

After several days of careful observation, Helen had a good idea of what to expect from one Martha Phelps. Any sort of partying was nowhere on the list.

Right on time, the jingly bunch of brass bells hanging over the front door rang out, and three perfectly normal-looking women walked in. Happy faces with just enough makeup to pass for fresh rather than fake. Carefully highlighted hair cut short or in a bouncy ponytail, jeans and tops as cheery as the chairs they'd soon gather in to chat.

Each carried big baskets stuffed full, with towels tucked in over the top. Even after watching them all week, Helen had no earthly idea how they could have so much laundry, day after day. She paid more than enough attention to know they weren't washing the same things like she was.

How could anyone *own* that many things, much less constantly need to wash them?

Kids at home, she supposed.

Neither she nor Rachel had wanted any, and sixteen years in, neither one regretted it. For one thing, Rachel often came along on these jobs if there was something fun for her to do.

Helen didn't blame her one bit for staying back in Atlanta for this one.

She smiled at the three women as she fed quarters into the throat of her washer, getting comfortable smiles in return. Being familiar always paid dividends on these small-town cases. As did pulling her dark brown hair (with the gray carefully removed) into a bouncy ponytail of her own.

Another two women came in, one with a basket, the other pushing what looked like a miniature shopping cart loaded up with clothes. Equally normal and friendly.

Still no Martha.

Helen forced herself to stay calm and as optimistic as the décor in the Lost Sock Laundry.

Even if her target on this job didn't show up tonight, there was always tomorrow. And the next day.

Please don't let this didn't stretch out to the weekend.

She started her clothes churning away and turned, meaning to arrange herself, her oversized chunky leather purse, and her required paperback of a recent bestseller close to where the women would gather.

Not *too* close, mind you, but enough that she could naturally join the conversation.

Before she took two steps, another woman opened the door and paused, a battered Army-green duffel bag slung over her shoulder. Brown sweatpants and a matching sweatshirt draped over a comfortable, matronly frame. Not a drop of makeup disguised her young-for-almost-seventy-face. Steel gray hair hung in waves past her shoulders, and eyes the same glinting gray took everything in before she walked through the door.

Those assessing eyes rested on Helen for a beat longer than on the guy way in the back, then her whole face lit at the sight of her friends. The warmth of her big smile and called-out greeting made it hard to believe she seemed so...suspicious only a second before.

Martha Phelps, on the scene at last.

Helen took a deep breath, blew out her tension,

and put her own suspicion firmly into the background. The game was finally on.

And she was more than ready to play.

By the time she made it to the front row of perky chairs, Helen had all the facts of the case fresh in her mind, yet held in the background. She memorized everything long before getting into a situation like this for damn good reason.

She settled in with her book, pleased to return hellos from two of the women.

Martha didn't say a word, but she jerked her chin toward Helen. Helen nodded back, then pretended to get into her book.

Under different circumstances, in another lifetime, she probably would have been friends with these women. But following the trail on a missing-person case the police had barely glanced at wasn't the time for friendship.

Anyway, Martha, with her quiet nature and mysterious past, was the next step on this trail.

Helen was determined to follow it to wherever Rodney Blevins had ended his days, no matter how it twisted or turned. Almost as determined as his family was to have their answers, even if no one else seemed to care.

She pretended to read and watched Martha load everything into one washer while everyone else was still busy sorting into two, sometimes three machines. All typical behavior for this crew.

But instead of standing around and chatting with her friends, Martha stared right at Helen.

Not good.

Then she walked over and sat beside her, which was worse.

"Figured I should introduce myself," Martha said, her voice quiet but a bit rough, as if she'd shouted a lot in her life. "Since we seem to have noticed each other for several days in a row now."

Helen smiled again, determined to salvage the situation. She adjusted the pattern and sound of her words to the local soft drawl.

"I'm sorry if I was staring. I've just had a lot on my mind. I think I scared someone in the produce department at the grocery store today doing exactly the same thing."

Martha nodded, pursing her lips. Up close her gray eyes had lovely highlights of green and gold.

"Hope you'll excuse me for saying so, but I don't buy you *not* paying attention to a damn thing. Not for one second, much less days in a row." She held out her hand. "Martha Phelps. Lived here most of my life. I work out at the warehouse at the railyard over in Banner."

Martha's hand was cool and rough, a lot like her voice, with a firm, confident grip.

"I'm glad to meet you, Martha. Gina Turnberry. I'm staying with my Aunt Shannon over in Steinman and her washer went out. I sure am sorry about staring like that."

Martha shook her head, but she still sat loose and relaxed, like she didn't have a care in the world. Helen on the other hand was doing her best not to tense up.

No one had recognized her or what she was doing for more years than she cared to admit.

In far more serious circumstances than chasing down a missing person exceedingly few people were likely to miss.

"Well, I have to say I appreciate you not whipping out too many details on that cover story, *Gina*. That or your fake ID, which I'm sure looks very official and all." Martha paused to give the slightest shake of her head toward one of the women walking toward them. The woman detoured toward another group of chairs instead.

"Not your fault, really," she said. You've been doing a fine job of fitting in. Better than most, even though I can hear you've lived away for a while in your accent. It's just that I've been watching out for folks like you since before you were born."

"I don't think I understand what—"

"Skip it." Martha frowned and shook her head slowly. "I've heard it all and then some. Police, sheriffs, feds, PIs. Doesn't matter. I think it would be a gesture of good faith if you show me your identification, though. That way I won't report you to the wrong bunch and waste both our time."

Helen closed her eyes for a second, debating her limited choices. She could continue to play ignorant and get out of here. Now. It wasn't like any of her clothes would be expensive to replace. But she had no doubt Martha would report her the second the jaunty bells above the door finished ringing. She'd get to the private investigator authorities soon enough.

Reciprocal licensing between Georgia and Virginia wouldn't stop word of Helen's little cut-and-run act from damaging her otherwise sterling reputation with her agency and state agencies alike.

She could flash that extremely good fake ID and hope for the best. Martha's cool gaze discouraged her on that course.

Instead, she pulled out her wallet, extracted her Georgia Bureau card, and handed it over. Revealing her stern face, real name, the firm she worked with, permit to carry, the works.

"You packing?" Martha said, glancing at the card before she returned it.

"Not today. Not on this job at all so far. The relevant authorities in Virginia know I'm operating here, and that I have a weapon available."

"I'm sure they do. I have my ideas, but you want to tell me what this is about now? I understand trying to get to the bottom of things, especially where a crime is concerned. Even if we may not agree on the definition of crime. If I can help you, I will."

Helen shrugged and shook her head at the same time. The *private* part of this investigation was blown. If she could still get what she needed, she'd happily put the family's worries to rest, collect her payment, and move on to better things.

"Okay then, Martha. Heard of Broken Ridge Mining?"

"Sure. Broken Ridge has been digging the mountains out under Laurel Gap and the whole county for over a hundred years now. Switched to taking the mountains down instead about ten years back. Half the town works for them. The other half understands where most of the money comes from."

Helen slipped her ID back into her wallet and tapped it on her thigh.

"Then maybe you heard about an incident back in October. A car accident."

"Heard plenty about it," Martha said, her eyes narrowing. "Late at night, patchy fog, roads slick, maybe icy in spots. Sweet little family coming home from a movie. Maybe not paying quite as much attention as they should be. Still, would have been hard to pay enough attention to avoid a three-ton boulder in the middle of a blind curve."

Helen clenched her jaws against the cold knots in her belly that felt as big as that rock.

She wasn't here to investigate what happened to that sweet little family. The police had handled that part quite well and in great detail.

Details she wished she'd never examined for herself.

"That's how it happened," she said. "Since you know that much, I'm going to guess you know how that night goes with Broken Ridge Mining."

Martha crossed her arms and sat back.

"I do. That road the family was driving down goes right alongside one of Broken Ridge's mining sites. One of their mountaintop removal sites, to be exact, so you might say it sort of goes *under* their operations. That night they were working on a road up top. An unpermitted road, as it turns out, not to mention after the hours they were supposed to be working. A couple of their heavy machinery folks weren't exactly experienced in road building, either."

"Thus the rock in the middle of the road."

"You got it, more or less. What I found interesting is how that rock sat there in the road for a solid hour, unreported. Just waiting for that car to meet up with it, end four lives, and tear up a great many more. No one up on that job site even seemed to know a thing was wrong until a man reporting to work got stopped by the backed-up traffic."

She raised one eyebrow and tilted her head.

"Hardly any traffic jams around here, you see. And when there are, it's a good bet the rescue squad is involved. They sure were busy that night. But I get the feeling you're not here to ask about that, are you?"

Helen forced her face to stay neutral, but she was scrambling to get a handle on where Martha was heading with all this. She had to know Broken Ridge Mining had been ordered to cease operations that night, and that substantial fines and ongoing investigations were in the works.

Was Martha as reasonably angry as everyone else in Laurel Gap was about what happened? Or did she actually know more than Helen's own investigation had already uncovered?

"No, Martha, I'm not here to ask you about that night, or the accident. I'm wondering if you know anything about Rodney Blevins."

The tension that had been hovering between them solidified.

Helen locked gazes with Martha, but all the movement and sound around them intensified. The guy way in the back started another dryer. The women up front raised their voices as they laughed and sang a few words of what sounded like a high school fight song.

The crackling dry air picked up a hit of something orange-scented, strong enough that Helen's mouth watered with craving.

"I know plenty about Rodney," Martha said. "His whole family, too. Damn shame the way he went missing and all."

"And what way was that? How he went missing? That's what I'm here to figure out."

Martha's cool expression finally gave way to a half-smile, but Helen didn't find it reassuring.

"You thinking I'm the one who finally put a stop to Rodney and his lifelong nonsense?"

"Nope. I haven't heard that at all. I *have* heard you might have a good idea who did."

Martha nodded and tucked her steel gray hair behind one ear.

"Now that's a refreshing change of pace. Your type is usually eager to pin all kinds of crap on me. I've been accused of more things in more places at more times than any single human being could possibly manage." Her smile widened for a second before it disappeared. "All while none of you seem to have the first clue what I might have *actually* been involved in."

Helen ignored the bright stab of curiosity of what an obviously tough-as-nails woman like Martha might be talking about. Especially if she truly had been watching out for investigators for nearly fifty years.

"I'm not accusing you of a thing. The only reason I'm here is to get to the bottom of what happened to Mr. Blevins."

"Any idea who's paying you to do that?" Martha said. "Or how the incident that night got linked up to Rodney in the first place? You're right about one thing. We didn't see all that much of an investigation of what happened to him for some strange reason."

"I'm aware of how quickly his disappearance seemed to slip under the law enforcement radar. I'm sure you know there was talk of Rodney working that night, but nothing proved that out no matter how hard the mine inspectors or the police tried. A concerned party asked me to get involved."

"A concerned party, huh?" Martha raised her eyebrow again. "Well, speaking as someone who knew that no-good boy his whole useless life, I can tell you not to trust anything you hear that shows he wasn't involved in a bad thing. And that no one in his family or in this town would honestly be concerned that he's gone. If that's who you think is writing your checks, you're badly mistaken, or maybe you've lived away too long."

A flash of annoyance verging on anger twisted through Helen, something that rarely happened to her on the job. The dismissive tone of Martha's words struck too close to her memories of home not far up the road. And to people she rarely ever saw, for very good reason.

"Okay then, let's say I have lived away too long. Never mind that I've got a hell of a lot of experience in research or that the source of payment has been verified. Who do you think is behind this whole thing?"

Martha lifted one shoulder and the corners of her mouth turned down.

"Hell, if the checks are big enough, I can personally guarantee no one who lives anywhere near here wrote 'em no matter what they claimed. Rodney's folks may very well have handed over your money. But you want to look up the line to who was paying *them*, and what for. In fact, I'd look up the mountain that family died beside."

"You think it was Broken Ridge Mining. What, because he was suspected of being on site that night? Or because he did grunt work for them a few months before he went missing? Nothing more than shoveling out under the belts and sweeping the floor from their records."

"I'm sure that's exactly what was in their records," Martha said slowly. "See, Rodney was the kind who hardly ever got paid on the record, for anything. I'm surprised it took this long for all he's done to catch up with him."

Helen took a deep breath, wishing the sharp orange scent hadn't faded away to more overly sweet florals. The guy in back had a neat stack of folded clothes in the chair beside him, and two of the women were unloading their underthings. One of them glanced toward Martha but didn't say a word.

"You know what happened to him," Helen said. "And who did it."

"I might at that."

"What you just said is enough for you to get called as a witness."

Martha snorted. "Is it now? Like you said earlier, law enforcement didn't much seem to care."

"Were you involved?"

"In shuffling him off this mortal coil? No ma'am, I was not."

"But you were involved in something to do with this."

"I've been involved in all kinds of things. Some

I'm proud of, some that make me sad. One or two I've regretted most of my life, and I expect to until I'm the one drawing my last. But what you're talking about now was nothing but me taking care of someone who did what had to be done."

"I'm not going to get into right or wrong here," Helen said. "That's not part of my job. I've dealt with some pretty nasty characters and uncovered things I wish I could forget. But I'm not here to pass judgement, or even to re-investigate the accident. All I'm after is what happened to Rodney Blevins. Nothing more, nothing less."

But images of those young parents, those two young kids hovered in her mind. Before, in a family portrait and vacation photos and school pictures.

And...after.

"Good." Martha startled her by smacking her own leg. "That's real good. Because I'm going to tell you what Rodney was doing when he dropped out of sight. Then you can make up your own mind what to do about it."

"What he was doing isn't important. That's not—"

"I'm going to tell you anyway. Then we'll see. Now, if you knew who to ask, and if they were willing to talk to you, you'd find out Rodney worked for more than one coal company. Couple of trucking outfits, a local quarry or two. Whoever needed his special skills. Not so much as a laborer, mind you. He never was much good at that. You might say Rodney was better suited for behind-the-scenes work."

She turned toward Helen and crossed her legs, clearly warming to her tale.

"Word is Rodney probably was up on the mountain that night, but no one would believe he had anything to do with that boulder finding its way down onto the road. Tragic and terrible as it was, the mine investigators got that one figured out for the most part. Where Rodney came in was making sure they didn't figure out the rest."

"Fine, I'll bite. What do you mean? He covered up for his boss?"

"I'm sure he would have if they paid him, if anyone would have believed a word he said. No, what Rodney did was encourage people who did know the truth to keep it to themselves. That's what he was good at, especially with a deep-pocketed company giving him the tools to do it with."

"You're saying he bribed witnesses to that boulder getting knocked down the mountain?"

Martha shook her head, her lips compressed into a straight line.

"No, I'm not saying that. Because like you pointed out, it's not what matters here. I'm saying he upset a lot of folks on behalf of his many employers over the years. Trying to get them to trade the health or even the lives of their loved ones for cash. Suggesting they take the money and leave it at that. No reporters, no lawyers. Sometimes people deep in grief take it out on the one standing in front of them rather than one that caused their pain. I'm sure you've heard of things like that. I figure Rodney knocked on the wrong door this time."

Helen shivered and didn't try to hide it. She had heard of things like that, a lot. The times that stayed with her were people getting notice of their kids or spouses dying in the military. The scars—physical and emotional—of her own father's service made the furious reactions all too easy to understand.

"You know what happened to him," she said. "And you're not going to tell me or anyone else. Is that about right?"

"That's about right. Not that anyone else to speak of has bothered to ask. Now you tell me something, Helen Hartsock. Do you think Rodney's people were truly looking for peace? Or were they just passing along the job and the check that went with it?"

Helen rubbed the back of her neck and glanced around the laundromat.

The guy in the back was folding his last load, his

closed laptop waiting patiently beside him. Martha's friends had all their loads in several dryers, including Martha's one mixed-up bunch.

And much to her surprise, Helen's own clothes now leapt and danced in two dryers rather than waiting for her in a sodden mass at the bottom of the washers.

One of the ponytailed women caught her gaze, nodded once, then went right back to chatting.

"To be more honest than I usually am," Helen said, "I got the impression Rodney's family was more concerned about *where* he is than what happened to him. I think they were...afraid to ask too many questions about that."

"I can work with that. And I can help you that much." Martha flashed her half-smile again, and this time it seemed more warm than cynical. "To be more honest than *I* usually am, I'm glad you weren't here to try to dig into my past. I like you, Helen. You seem more sensible than most in your line of work. Maybe even sensible enough to get your information and let this one go."

"What, because it all came out right in the end or something like that?"

This time, Martha smacked Helen's knee, hard enough to sting a bit.

"Because it all came out right in the end. With

the local coverup con artist out of the picture, a whole lot more things are likely to turn out right around here. I say that can only be a good thing."

Helen wrote down the location, deeper into the steep wooded terrain than she would have imagined. Deep enough that the unknown person's heartbreak, fury, and determination to right a terrible wrong in some way came through loud and clear.

Even in the clean, bright, cheerful yellow and pink of The Lost Sock Laundromat.

"And if someone else comes asking the same questions?" Helen said. "Paid by the same concerned party?"

The way Martha's eyes flashed promised more trouble than Helen cared to pursue.

"I've said all I'm going to about Rodney. Anyone else who comes around won't get nearly so far. Or nearly so friendly."

"Makes sense to me."

"So now you got all you need. And we're all clear."

Helen nodded. Her mind served up the smiling faces of that young family now, rather than the end of them. She was grateful for that much.

In this case at least, it would have to be enough.

"We're all clear. As far as I'm concerned, this is

all anyone needs to know about that night. I appreciate you telling me."

Helen started to get up, then flashed her own lopsided smile. "You can probably guess what I want to ask, even though I have a feeling you won't tell me."

Martha shook her head as she got to her feet, but her eyes were amused.

"You're right, and I won't. All I'll tell you is it really was before you were born, from the date I saw on your ID. And no one got hurt or died. I intend to take that little adventure to my grave, wherever that turns out to be. That's about when the statute of limitations will run out, anyway."

"Fair enough. Thank you, Martha. You take care of yourself."

"Same to you, Helen. Same to you."

Martha turned and joined her friends waiting beside the front door. As they walked out together, each woman looked Helen in the eye. Just for a second, but enough to make an impression. The guy in the back had slipped out without her noticing.

Helen gathered up her neatly folded clothes, thankfully not smelling of anything fruity or flowery.

She thought of Rachel back in Atlanta. Of their friends, closer than Helen's own family not that far down the road. Of how all those women might have been related to Martha, maybe.

But whether they were related or not, they were obviously her true and solid friends.

Like she suspected the nameless person who'd finally stopped Rodney Blevins from walking the earth had been.

Helen hoped her own friends felt that way about her, even though heaven forbid they ever had to go that far. That old joke about true friends helping you hide the body didn't seem quite as funny to her as it used to.

And she hoped she'd be strong enough to go that far, just as much as she hoped she never needed to.

JASON A. ADAMS

Author of *To Catch a Thief* and *If You're There*

DISCOVERING THE OBVIOUS

For all of us who never know flirting when we see it.

CHAPTER 1

For Sheriff Larry Crabtree, some things stayed true year in and year out.

For instance, a man ought to be nice and friendly to gate agents at the airport. Those folks took a world of grief day after day, and when a feller smiled and said howdy, he might just get a better seat.

Or how about looking both ways before you cross the street? Seemed like one any fool didn't need to be told, but he and his deputies scraped up one or two boneheads every year from the far Southwestern Virginia streets and back roads.

His favorite truism, though, was one he'd learned from his great-granny Pearlie when he'd been knee high to a grasshopper.

Ain't nothin' in life so bad that fresh-baked cookies can't make it better.

Larry sat in the kitchen of the old homeplace he'd inherited from Granny Pearlie, reading through the notes his deputy Joan Foyle had written up on Jessie Holbrook, the most recent headache riding a morgue slab in town. Between his feet, his redbone hound Skinner snored away. Outside, the sun kicked sparks off a few inches of last night's snow.

He couldn't hardly concentrate. A rich warm smell of roasted nuts, cinnamon, and brown sugar kept trying to seduce him away from work. The aroma went straight up his nose and down to his belly, teasing him with the promise of happiness to come.

Larry wasn't much for colored lights or tinsel or any of that rickrack. Baked goodies were all the Christmas decoration he needed.

The battered old table currently serving as desk was made of time-worn maple boards three inches thick and scarred with the marks of many a battle between Granny's cleaver and whatever poor animal sat in for dinner.

Larry had renovated most of the house, bringing in running water and electric, double-paned windows, a modern enamel-steel roof instead of the old rusty tin sheets, along with other comforts and updates.

But he hadn't touched her kitchen a bit, except to

replace the ancient wood-fired stove with a new propane range. This room more than anywhere else in the world was where Granny still lived for him.

Especially when it smelled of lovin' from the oven, like now.

Larry wouldn't ever be the cook the old lady was, but he'd studied on what she did quite a bit when he'd been a boy. She didn't think it strange that a boychild wanted to learn his way around the pots and pans, and he'd spent plumb near every summer riding her apron strings, learning how to fill bellies while she filled his head with all the old stories and old lore.

The timer dinged and Larry stood, stretched, and pulled on the threadbare oven mitts that still lived on cut-nails driven into the log wall behind the stove. Granny'd sewed them herself sometime back before cars had radios.

He opened the door and sucked in as much of the blast of peanut butter and molasses as he could, eyes watering from the heat, mouth watering from pure ol' cookie lust.

He'd barely had time to set the pan of goodness on the sideboard to cool when his radio blipped from the chair where he'd hung his utility belt. Two short, two long. Joan, asking for a callback. The sorta-Morse code meant she wanted phone, not radio. Fewer ears and scanners listening in.

Ah, hell. He had a few minutes while things cooled down.

Larry pulled his trusty iPhone from his pocket and dialed. Joan picked up right away.

"Hey, boss. Need to holler at you. Got a bad one."

"Hey, Joanie. I'm readin' your report right now. Just gimme—"

"Forget about Jessie. That damn fool got drunk and kissed his windshield and then an oak tree when he ran his truck off the road. I need you to come out to Kyle Meade's place."

Kyle? He'd just seen the old root-digger out to town yesterday. Seemed spry as a squirrel.

"What's happened?"

"Just come on, hon. You can catch up on all the gossip when you get here."

She killed the call. Joanie'd been curt and quarrelsome for a week. Ever since her cousin Paul up and took off, leaving her stuck with the rent on the house they shared. Best not to tick her off. Joan could take Larry eight times in ten in the sparring ring.

In spite of—or maybe because of—her powerful build and ability to muscle even the meanest drunks and addicts into the back of her prowler by herself,

Larry'd regretted more than once that she was his deputy and therefore off-limits.

Didn't hurt that she was sharp as a tack and had a great head for the work.

Joanie had a degree in criminal justice and could probably do a lot better than his shabby little department. She'd been involved with the Commonwealth Bureau of Criminal Investigation and the Drug Enforcement Services on a couple of major pot and meth busts. Joanie tried to pass the credit up to Larry, but he made her take all of it.

The county was too small for him to justify paying a detective, but if he did get one, he'd want Joanie.

Which meant she wasn't just blowing smoke. Something out of the ordinary had her back up, and he better go see.

Larry sighed, cast a wistful eye over the cooling pan, risked his fingers and tongue enough to shove two gooey comforters in his mouth, and reached for Skinner's leash and his gun belt.

CHAPTER 2

Larry wished he were somewhere else. Anywhere else.

He stood in the middle of Kyle's house, a snug collection of six rooms, if you counted the bathroom. A plain square building, with no pretensions.

The sitting room was one of the two original rooms, built of waist-thick chestnut logs nearly a century ago by Kyle's great-granddad. A lumpy horsehair sofa with the sort of dung-toned coarse-weave upholstery that should've been outlawed sat beneath two narrow windows. Tobacco-stained walls nearly as brown as the couch held framed photos of Kyle and Jeannette. On their honeymoon, at Myrtle Beach, standing out in the front yard. Normal, happy couple.

The snow outside looked ghostly through the elderly rippled window panes.

Warmth filled the space, both from the ancient bruise-colored coal stove, and from the crowd. Joan stood beside Doc Phipps, a steel-haired veteran of countless childbirths and heart attacks. Two inches taller and probably forty pounds heavier, Joan looked like his bodyguard. Mahogany hair pulled back in a long ponytail should have softened her edges, but only made her look tougher.

The Doc was also the Dickenson County coroner, when he wasn't sewing up cuts and listening to hearts beat through his stethoscope. His assistant Tommy leaned against the wall, picking at his nails with a penknife, trying to look more bored than pukey. Two uniformed techs from the State Police forensics division picked through overflowing ashtrays, a trashcan full of PBR corpses, and a book-shelf full of naughty Stuckey's knickknacks.

Trashy things probably be worth a fortune on eBay, if you could find someone who couldn't do without a tiny flasher hiding in an outhouse.

Bright, multi-colored flashes blinked on and off from the tinsel-wrapped Christmas tree, set in the opposite corner from the blazing coal fire, thank goodness. On top of the stove, a pot full of homemade potpourri filled the air with citrus and spices, valiantly trying to cover a heavy, coppery reek.

The place was busting with holiday cheer, but the effect was spoiled by all the law.

And by the dead man in the room.

"What do you think, Larry?" Doc Phipps asked.

Larry stopped telling himself he was examining the scene, and looked down at the braided rag rug. The forest green and burgundy loops held a wide patch of dark wetness, pooling out from what was left of Kyle Meade's head.

"I think Kyle's dead, Doc. What do *you* think?" Larry didn't much like the sharpness in his voice. The doc had been his friend for years, and his own doctor since diaper days.

Doc Phipps didn't flinch. He'd been around dead folks and tense cops plenty.

"Well, my good sheriff. In my professional opinion, based on years of education and experience in the medical field, I'd say someone bashed Kyle's head in with a blunt object. Possibly a baseball bat."

The old man was plumb full of wit. Joan was right then marking a blood-stained 34-inch Rawlings into evidence.

"How you want to play it, boss?" Joan asked. She didn't have any evidence bags big enough for the bat, so it sat in a white kitchen Hefty, among a growing pile of red-labeled sealables.

"Let's get out on the porch," Larry said. "Give the staties time to do their work."

They went out and sat in the two bentwood rockers. One was Kyle's. The other for his wife Jeannette, gone these past eight years. Kyle had pretty much kept himself to himself after she passed from gut cancer. He spent most of his time up on the mountain, grubbing for ginseng, bloodroot, anything he could make a few bucks on. He only came into town to sell his findings and buy groceries.

The old man—old...he was five years older than Larry—didn't cause any fuss. Neither Larry nor his two deputies had ever so much as pulled him over for an expired sticker. Quiet and lonesome. He'd had more grooves in his face than his years called for, and carried an air of guilt and remorse with him.

Pining for the wife he couldn't save, folks said.

"Anyone check Kyle's truck?" he asked, looking over at the blue and rust Chevy parked in the yard.

"Nothing there but his ' sang stick," she said.

They sat quietly for a while. Inside, the scuffles and mutters of the forensics team alternated with the occasional *snap* of the oversized evidence camera.

It just don't make no sense, Larry thought. Kyle wasn't an angel, but he sure wasn't any kind of devil, either. He was just ol' Kyle Meade. Not much of a drinker, but made the best cold medicine around. Made his own white whiskey for it, but didn't sell ' shine. Didn't suffer fools or punk kids, but never did more than yell at them to "git home to momma ' fore I whup the skin off yore seat."

Might someone do for him over a woman? Not likely. Since Jeannette, Kyle stayed away from the opposite sex. Many a well-meaning lady had tried to fix him up, but he'd look at them with those haunted eyes of his until they let him alone.

Finally, the forensics boys came out, followed by Doc Phipps and Tommy, wheeling a sheet-covered hump on the gurney.

Ain't no mistakin' a stiff on a sled.

Joan and Larry stood respectfully as the Doc supervised loading the body into the converted Blazer that served as ambulance and hearse for the more isolated homesteads. Tommy secured a set of straps, lashing the gurney in place, then slammed the rear doors.

"That's me done," Doc said, coming over to shake Larry's hand. "I'll get him back to the hospital, run all the usual tox screens, check his BAC, but I don't think I'll find anything. Kyle's position on the floor and some splatter on the walls says he was standing up, at least when he took the first lick. Back of the head's worse than the front, so I doubt he was facing the Babe when he started swinging."

"What makes you think the killer was male?" Joan asked.

Doc gave her a look. "You see the shape, or shapelessness, his head was in? You're a plenty big girl and I wouldn't arm-wrestle you, but I don't think you could have caused that much damage without wearing yourself out."

Larry saw Joan start to swell, and jumped in before she decided to prove the Doc wrong. Joan and her cousin Paul had gone to State every year they'd been eligible. Him for baseball, her for fast-pitch soft-ball. She still held a passel of county records for batting and fielding. Paul only had four. Home runs by a varsity freshman, sophomore, junior, and senior.

"Come on, Deputy Foyle," Larry said, taking her arm. "Let's you and me get back to the office and get the paperwork done.

CHAPTER 3

Twenty minutes later, he and Joan sat in his office in the Holly Creek municipal building. Which was nothing but the county courthouse. The new consolidated regional jails had freed up a bunch of floor space, so all the government offices had moved in here. Holly Creek town had the upstairs, Dickenson County had the down.

Larry took a stack of messages from Pauline, his young receptionist. She was breaking dress code with that silly pointed elf hat of hers, but Larry let it slide. Again. At least he'd talked her out of slingin' garlands all about the place.

He put the coffee pot on, and Joan moved a stack of files off his visitor's chair before sitting down. He plopped behind his desk, turning to the window to see how Skinner was getting by out in the little dog run he'd built out back. Being Sheriff did have a couple of perks.

"Heard from Paul?" he asked, turning back to his deputy.

"No, I haven't," she said, blowing a lock of hair back where it'd snuck out of her ponytail. "It's not like him to take off without leaving word. Not like…" Which was as close as the no-nonsense deputy would come to admitting she was worried.

Joanie scowled and looked away. Some folks would think her angry, but Larry knew better.

She and Paul had grown up together, along with Paul's little sister Julie. Their folks had been killed by a drunk coal truck driver who crossed the yellow line and crushed their Subaru like tinfoil. Paul and Julie had been with Joanie's family, and stayed on after. Joan and Paul had both been heartbroken when Julie ran out on her husband Mark seven years ago. No note, no message, just vanished. They all still believed she was alive out there somewhere, and would be in touch when she got through whatever drove her off.

Trouble follows some families.

"He'll turn up," Larry said. "Probably off after deer or turkey." He opened a desk drawer and pulled a blank incident report from the stack inside.

"Well, we might as well get started," he said.

"Mind if I write while you talk? It'll help set things in my head."

"I don't mind a bit, Lar," she said. "You have better handwriting anyway."

"So who found Kyle?"

"I did," she said. "Somebody stuck a note under the door sometime this morning. All it said was we needed to go check Kyle's place."

Joan took a folded piece of white paper from her pants pocket and handed it over. The message inside matched Joanie's statement. The smooth black letters had been made by a laser printer, not typed or hand-written.

"Already check it for prints?"

"Of course I did, papa," she said. "I'm a good girl, remember?"

Larry snorted.

"Okay, good girl. Until forensics come back, we can't do much except hit the road and ask around. Maybe grab some lunch, my treat."

"Why, Sheriff Crabtree. Are you asking me on a date?" Joan batted her eyes at him like a cartoon character.

"Sorry, Joanie. You know the rules about fraternization. You driving?"

"Only if we take your car," she said, smiling. "I don't want a bunch of dog hair messing up my seats."

They stood and left the office, chuckling. Larry wondered if Joan regretted the rules the way he did. But it was better that way. Kept things simple. He tried to stay out of his deputies' private lives, so long as they stayed out of each others'.

CHAPTER 4

What a waste of time.

After hours of driving up and down the ridges and hollers, they weren't any closer to a motive, let alone a suspect. The sun dropped, and the temperature followed, the clear sky full of bright stars and empty of warmth.

"I'm beat, Boss," Joanie said when they got back to the office. "I'm off to my bathtub and my bed. Gonna enjoy the privacy while my house is empty. See you back here at eight?"

Larry couldn't help a quick glance when Joanie got out of the car and stretched tall, arching her back with her hands clasped behind her head. Her brown shirt slipped loose of her britches, and a thin line of creamy skin peeked out.

Larry snapped his head back so fast he figured a neck crick was in his future.

"I'll be here earlier than that, most likely," he said, rubbing his cheeks to cover the heat he felt there. "But you don't have to get out in the cold until your time. Be safe going home, Joanie."

She leaned down to look at him through her open door. She opened her mouth, then shut it with a little laugh and shook her head.

"Have a good night, Sheriff. Keep yourself warm." With that, she waved and walked out to her own prowler.

Now what was that all about?

Larry put it out of his mind. Not easy, considering that little flash of belly button. He had more important things to worry about, dammit.

"Come on, boy," he said to his snoring hound dog in back. "Let's get on back and get a bite."

His mind worried at Kyle's death the whole way back home. Larry went through his evening routine without seeing it, straining to come up with anybody who might have a grudge against Kyle. He opened the freezer, took out a frozen dinner without seeing it, and threw it in the microwave.

Larry paced the kitchen floor while he waited on his supper, around and around his granny's old butcher-block table. Skinner clicked along behind him, occasionally shoving his furry head under Larry's hand.

"I'm sorry, boy," he said, stopping to give the hound a proper ear skritching. "I been ignorin' you, haven't I? Tell ya what. Because I feel bad, you get half my dinner. Sound good?"

Skinner only groaned as Larry's fingers worked his ears, big brown pleading hound dog eyes slowly closing.

The microwave dinged, and Larry retrieved the plastic Swanson's tray.

Lasagna with meat sauce and mozzarella cheese. Larry looked down at the white and red mess, and his traitorous mind served up the bloody remains of Kyle Meade's head.

In the end, Skinner got the whole thing.

Larry took a stiff shot of Pepto, chased it with warm milk, and went to bed. It wasn't late yet, but this day deserved an early end. Hopefully the state boys would have something by tomorrow.

CHAPTER 5

L arry walked into the kitchen, the scuffed Keds on his feet slapping the plain floorboards. A wonderful aroma of chicken and dumplings, soup beans, and cornbread filled his nostrils.

He looked down at himself and saw the little boy he'd once been, and smiled.

Must be a vistin' night.

He ran to the table and hopped up into one of the worn chairs. His elbows went on the freshly-scrubbed table, his chin went on his hands, and he waited.

Granny Pearlie, wearing the blue calico dress and sunbonnet he always saw her in, puttered at the ancient wood-burning cookstove, stirring this, flipping that, adding a smidge of extra to the other.

"I hope you ain't expectin' me to steer ye on this

one, Lar-Bear," she said, her back still to him. She stirred the beans, took a taste from the long wooden spoon, and threw in another pinch of salt.

"But Granny, you *always* know how to fix things."

The old woman turned to him, one hand on a broad hip while the other took her old corncob pipe from her apron pocket. She struck a blue-tip on the side of the stove and drew the flame into the pipe's bowl.

"Always is a right long time, Lar-Bear, but never mind that. You got two problems, but you only see the one." She shook the match as she sat down opposite Larry. "Ain't nobody tryin' to hide what happened out to Kyle Meade's this mornin', they just ain't talked yet.

"Now your *other* problem, which ain't much of a problem a'tall for anybody's got a lick o' sense, is one you might could actually do somethin' about," she said, tapping his forehead with a bony finger, "if you take a come-along and prize your eyes open."

"What other problem, Granny?" He was just a kid, and she was scaring him. "What's happened? Please tell me!"

"Sorry, Lar-Bear," she said. "Some things are best left 'twixt those involved. I'll give ye a hint on your first trouble, though. Ask them other fellers what were at Kyle's with ye whether they looked down in the can cellar."

"Why? What's down there?"

But the old woman just blew out a cloud of blue smoke, laughed, and faded out, taking the kitchen with her.

CHAPTER 6

Aloud pounding jolted Larry awake. In bed. He was in his bed. Skinner had jumped down and run to the kitchen, barking his head off. Not his usual machine-gun alarm, but the excited *yarks* that told Larry a friend was outside.

"Gimme a damn minute," he mumbled to himself as the banging outside kept on.

Pants.

Pants on the chair.

He got up, rubbing his eyes as a gigantic yawn sent his chin climbing down his chest. Undershirt would have to do. He managed to get his pants on, and shoved his feet into a pair of dark brown pleather slippers. Old fart shoes, but comfortable.

Larry made it to the kitchen and switched on the

coffee pot before heading to the door. Good thing the boards were so thick. Someone on the other side was playing some serious jackhammer.

"What the hell is it?" he yelled, grabbing Skinner's collar and pulling him back so he could yank the door open. "You don't got to beat my damn door—"

Joanie stood on the stoop, right hand still raised in a fist. Her eyes were wide and scared. Her face bone-pale, except for bright strawberries high on her cheeks. Larry didn't think he'd ever seen that look on her stolid face. A piece of paper stuck out of a spiral notebook in her left hand.

"What is it, Joan honey?" Larry said in what he hoped was a calm voice. "You come inside and sit. I've got coffee going. Come on now." He took her arm and pulled her gently but firmly inside. He'd been an MP in the Army for years before returning to Dickenson County and the sheriff's job, and had plenty of experience with people who had just been dealt a shock bad enough to cause a short-circuit.

He got Joanie settled at the table with a steaming mug of black coffee in front of her. She grabbed it with both shaking hands and took several large gulps.

"It's Paul, Larry," she said when she finally put the mug down. "Paul and Julie and...oh God!" Joan,

Larry's tough and efficient deputy, put her face in her hands and began to weep.

Larry patted her shoulder awkwardly. What in the world was going on?

"What about Paul, Joanie? Is he in trouble? Is he in the hospital or something? He finally hear from Julie?"

"Yeah, kinda," she said, her sobs turning into a frightening giggle. "Oh yeah. He heard quite a lot from Julie." She handed the notebook to Larry. "Spot's marked."

Larry kept an eye on Joan as he took the notebook. The shock was slowly leaving her eyes, probably because she had someone to share whatever was in this book with.

The notebook had a plain green cover. Larry had seen ones just like it most every day. This kind came from the Rite-Aid in town, two for a dollar.

Inside, the pages were filled margin to margin with neat handwriting in purple ink. Purple. Wasn't that Julie's favorite color?

Larry started to read, one hand still on Joanie's shoulder. Skinner gave him a hand by putting his head in her lap. Joan automatically reached down to rub his ears. Ear rubs were the best medicine in the world, for giver and receiver.

What he read made him cross to the other chair and fall into it.

The notebook was Julie's diary. Part of it anyway. The first page was dated January 22, the year she disappeared. Mostly she wrote about day-to-day stuff...dinner plans, town gossip, ideas for vacations, and so on.

Larry scanned to the middle of the book, where Julie started to write about trouble with her husband Mark. Larry hadn't heard of any problems, and Mark had thought at the time they'd been getting along just fine.

But Julie wrote about boredom, about feeling like Mark took her for granted...

About how Kyle Meade talked to her when they were at the laundry-mat together. How he wanted to hear all about her day, about her life. How lonely the older man was now that his wife was gone.

How she started to feel things for Kyle she hadn't felt for a long time with Mark. How she planned to go to Kyle's house and surprise him. See how he really felt about her. She'd wear her prettiest clothes, and some perfume she'd just bought. And the amethyst earrings which had been her favorite since middle school.

"'Wish me luck, Dear Diary!' was the last entry.

Larry read the words a second time. Then a

third. Could Mark have known? He looked up to ask Joan, and saw she was watching him. She seemed calmer now. Still a little pale, but with more color than she'd had.

"Read the note," she said, still rubbing Skinner's head.

Larry looked down at what stuck out between the notebook's pages. An envelope. Larry took a sheet of paper from it, opened it, and read.

It was handwritten, in the sloppy scrawl of someone in a hurry. Or with a lot on their mind.

I found Julie.

Sorry I couldn't tell you before I left, but you would have stopped me and I couldn't let that happen to Sis. I found her diary in a bunch of stuff I was helping Mark get out of the garage. I guess he didn't read any of it. Don't tell him, okay? His heart's broke enough.

Check that bastard's basement. I left Julie there. God forgive me, but I couldn't let anyone know until I fixed things. I love you, Cuz. I'm sorry, but I hope you understand.

P.

P for Paul. Home Run Champion four years running.

The note was written on Dickenson County Sheriff's Department letterhead. The envelope was postmarked priority overnight, from Nogales, Arizona.

The Mexican border.

Larry looked at Joan, who returned his gaze. She'd passed beyond shock to anger, judging by the clenched jaw and narrowed brows.

"Let's go," they said together.

CHAPTER 7

Kyle's living room was again crowded with lawmen and medical folk. There wasn't enough room in the cellar for everybody.

Larry and Joanie had gone down in the basement to find a patch of freshly disturbed earth under a tarp.

Twenty years' worth of Mason jars watched on as Larry and Joan dug carefully with their blue gloved hands, until Larry felt something hard and smooth beneath his fingers.

A skull.

Another minute of digging revealed the separated vertebrae of a broken neck.

Larry went outside to call in support while Joanie guarded the hole. They'd stopped digging when a tiny purple earring in a green-tarnished setting showed beside the fleshless head.

They needed to let the forensics squad finish unearthing the body, but neither Larry nor Joanie had any doubts. No doubts about the identity, and no doubts about who killed Kyle Meade.

Larry sat on the edge of the porch and called the local airport had revealed that yes, Paul Foyle's Jeep was in the short term lot. If the family could come claim it today, the attendant wouldn't have to call a tow truck.

As for Julie and Kyle? Larry wondered what really happened that day seven years ago. Did Kyle murder Julie? Did she fall down the stairs? Slip in the bathroom?

"I guess we'll never know," Joanie said, sitting beside Larry and echoing his thoughts. "If Paul ever gets in touch, I can ask what he knows, but..."

She'd been crying again, but Larry didn't fault her none.

"Poor Julie," Larry said, absently putting his arm around Joanie's shoulders. "Whatever happened, I hope she didn't hurt none."

He noticed where his arm was and jumped, pulling himself up and away from his deputy. Forget his face, his whole head was on fire.

"I, uh, we that is, I mean *I* should get back," he said, stumbling all over his own tongue. "You can supervise all this, can't you?"

"Sure, boss," she said. Her eyes were still red-ringed and damp, but for some reason she was smiling. "You go on ahead. I'll catch up."

CHAPTER 8

Three days after her skeleton was released from the forensic investigation, Julie Foyle was buried in the Holly Creek Memorial Gardens, beside her mom and dad. A few cousins and old friends attended the funeral, along with Mark.

While he would need some quality time with a good therapist to work through all the unknowns, Mark seemed like a load had been lifted.

At least he knew where his wife was now.

The investigation into Julie's demise was quick and to the point. Death by dislocation between C_3 and C_4. Lack of remaining soft tissue made anything more exact impossible.

The hunt was still on for Kyle's murderer, but the Dickenson County Sheriff's Office wouldn't be doing much of it. As far as Larry was concerned, the whole nightmare just needed to be over. Neither Paul nor Kyle had any family left, Joanie finally knew the truth, so who would get the closure everyone talks about?

Larry and his deputies were back to getting drunks and drag racers off the road, serving various warrants and summonses, running people out of illegal deer stands, all the exciting work of a rural cop's life. Larry didn't mind. In his line of work, he preferred boring over exciting any day of the week.

He was going through the day's mail when one envelope caught his eye. It was addressed to him personally, and there was no stamp or postmark. No return address, either.

Larry tore the envelope open, a heavy feeling down in his gut. What now?

The envelope held a short letter, handwritten on blue steno pad paper.

Larry shot up and tore out the door, yelling as he went.

"Joan! Joanie! Joan Foyle, where the *hell* are you at??"

"Right here, boss. Why?" Joanie said. She was at her desk, feet up on her blotter, reading a Lee Child novel. She had that innocent look only the cheerfully guilty are capable of.

"What the hell is this?" Larry shouted, waving

the letter under her nose. "I mean, just what the hell *is* this?"

"You really should get some reading glasses, man your age," Joanie said, smirking. "What does it look like? I quit, effective five this afternoon."

"But I thought you liked being a cop," Larry said. Joanie couldn't leave. He—the *department* needed her! "What did I—what can I do to change your mind?"

"Nary a thing, big boy," she said. She was flat out grinning now.

Larry had a mind to...

Joan handed him another letter. This one much more official looking, with a fancy blue letterhead with big official looking seals and important sounding names.

Larry snatched it out of her hand.

Un-friggin'-believable.

"The BCI?" he said, throwing the letter down. "The damn state police? You're leaving me to be a goddamn *statie*?"

"Sure am, Boss," she said, getting to her feet and coming around the desk. "I got a job in the Drug Enforcement Division. They're so happy with me after last year's meth lab busts, they even let me pick my post. I'll be fifteen miles away, in the Wise County Field Office."

"Well, fine. Good for you, I guess," Larry grumbled. It *was* good for her, a fantastic career opportunity. He should be happy for her. Shouldn't he? "Merry Christmas, Joanie. I'm right proud of ya."

"You know what this means, don't you?" she said, coming closer.

"Means I gotta find a new—"

"What it *means*, you big dummy," she said, putting a finger on his lips, "is that fraternization no longer applies."

Larry's eyes bugged plumb out when she replaced her finger with her own lips.

It might just be a merry Christmas after all.

He didn't even hear Pauline and the rest of the office cheering them on.

It might just be a merry Christmas after all.

KARI KILGORE

AUTHOR OF INTO THE STORM AND SONGS IN THE MOUNTAIN

ADVENTURES IN WINTER DRIVING

A Storms of Future Past Story

*For everyone who's ever driven
down a snowy mountain road*

Wondering if they should have stayed home.

ADVENTURES IN WINTER DRIVING

Carol Sanderson had the strangest feeling of sitting inside a huge snow globe that just got a good, hard shake.

The world outside the windows of her trusty Jeep Liberty was overlaid in sparkling white. Huge snowflakes danced and spun on their way down—a sure sign of the end of mid-December's oddly warm and rainy weather.

She switched the Jeep's heater from full defrost to sending a stream of warm air toward her hands, and especially her feet. Her toes weren't cold yet, not through her heavy winter boots and thick wool socks. But it didn't hurt a bit to fend off the coming assault.

A strong whiff of coffee and hot chocolate floated through the car as soon as the front vents kicked in.

Right over the cupholders where she'd put two stainless steel mugs-full.

A sip of steaming-hot heavenly brew chased away the lingering chill.

The heater's dry air and the maroon knit cap she had pulled low over her ears were guaranteed to send her hair into a floaty auburn halo. Couldn't be helped. She'd rather be a bit fuzzy than freezing later on.

About the only thing she could see besides all that gorgeous white was a yellowish glow outside her passenger side window. The porch light of her boyfriend Sid Rutherford's house.

Probably warm and cozy inside, sliding toward much too warm if her past experience proved right. She could go wait in there, certainly. Save a little gasoline. Avoid putting a little pollution into the chilly late afternoon air.

Sit through yet another round of puzzled looks and questions from his sweet and incredibly confusing parents. To be fair, they were probably every bit as confused by their son and the stubborn, feisty woman he kept bringing home for dinners and holidays.

Carol could just about write the script after two years of dating Sid.

Why are you out on a day like this? Did you fill

up your gas tank? Are your tires in good shape? Is your cell phone charged? Are you wearing warm socks? And of course: Carol dear, I don't think Miss Kellen would mind one bit if you and Sid called off work just this one time, do you?

As if her thoughts summoned electrons out of the snow, her smartphone buzzed.

So sorry, C. Getting winter driving rundown from M&D. Out there ASAP. S.

Carol snorted and glanced at the porch light again. That was an awful lot of typing with Sid's big fingers even on his own pocket computer. She was quite impressed he'd managed it mid-parental lecture.

She couldn't imagine trying such a trick after years of experience with her own parental lectures. Her father would catch her in a heartbeat.

Five years of experience driving up and down the steep, winding mountain road to Maple Ridge had her convinced she'd do just fine getting them to work and back, no matter what Sid's parents said.

Well, five years *legally* driving. Like pretty much everyone else in such a remote location with no hospital or rescue squad or police presence to speak of, Carol's behind-the-wheel education started years before the Commonwealth of Virginia would have approved. The realities of having to make it over half an hour down a gorgeous but extremely twisty mountain road to Wolf Branch for any sort of help overrode a lot of fear of bending the law.

A hard gust of wind sent a spray of snow pattering against the driver side window, and sent Carol to superstitiously amending her confidence in her driving skills.

She was confident in her ability to drive as long as the road didn't ice *and* no trees blocked the way. If either of those things happened, she'd calmly make other arrangements, even if it meant going home early or calling for help.

There. The gods of winter (and the specter of parents warning her to be careful) appeased and hopefully satisfied.

Carol had just pulled off one of her gloves to tap out a quick reply to Sid when he materialized through the snow, opened the door, and folded his lanky self into the passenger seat, bringing a burst of cold air and frustration with him.

"I'm so sorry, Carol, making you wait like this. It was everything I could do to get out the door. They were asking me why you couldn't come inside and have some hot apple cider so we could all talk it over."

He stared at her under the harsh dome light, and she got the same crazy flock-of-delirious-birds sensation in her belly as the first time she saw him. Thick black hair, wavy enough to capture an impressive sample of snowflakes. Big blue eyes, annoyed and apologetic at the same time.

He hadn't stopped to zip up his puffy green jacket on the way out, so his faded Maple Ridge Maple Barn sweatshirt was nearly as snowy as his head.

Carol smiled, then lost her battle to suppress a laugh. She leaned over to kiss his cold cheek before putting the Jeep in gear.

"Gave you a good interrogation, did they?"

Sid rolled his eyes just before the dome light winked out.

"Yeah, they were on a solid roll. Mom had the phone in hand to call Miss Kellen and explain why we simply could not *possibly* go out there tonight and put up her tree, no matter what tradition dictates. Oh, and I most sincerely *promised* to be sure to ask you if you have your car in four-wheel drive."

The smile she heard in his voice kept Carol from getting annoyed. At the question itself, a little.

Also that she hadn't included that inquiry in her inner dramatization of parental interrogation.

"Not yet, my dear Mr. Rutherford." She tapped the smaller shifter knob beside the main gearshift in the console between them with a short fingernail.

"The roads are perfectly clear, you see. The snow is melting everywhere that counts, and my tank of a vehicle tells me it's still thirty-eight degrees out there. Four-wheel drive would only put an unnecessary and unhelpful strain on my transmission."

As she generally did, Carol spoke the truth, even where neither her parents or Sid's could hear her. Snow collected on the trees, sidewalks, and parked cars of the residential neighborhood. Those huge gorgeous flakes melted as soon as they landed on the asphalt, probably because abnormally warm weather and torrents of rain kept the roads warm and damp.

Sid imitated his father's slow cadence and almost sing-song accent perfectly, and affectionately.

"Now I'd never want to question your driving skill, Carol, but I sure don't know about that. You can never be too safe with these kinds of things on a day like this."

Carol blew a raspberry at him as she turned down Maple Ridge's Main Street. In a break in the snow and under bright street lights on earlier than usual, they could see several cars and trucks—and more than a few Jeeps—still in front of the shops and in the parking lot of the Maple Barn.

"Then may I point out how many of our fellow citizens are out shopping?" she said. "And I'd bet every single person in the criminally overpriced

Maple Barn is from somewhere far away. They'll still have to make their way down a hundred and one turns off this mountain. Anyway, Miss Sandra Kellen simply *must* have her Christmas tree before the winter solstice and her cozy party. We're about to run out of days."

Carol took the last left, before Main Street turned into Route 828 and headed down the back side of the mountain and out of town. Only one more house remained in Maple Ridge, and it was the reason the town existed in the first place.

The Grand Old Kellen Place.

And yes, the capital letters were always, always there.

"I tried to tell them it's not even supposed to snow a foot." Sid took a long drink of his coffee, then stared out into the darkening afternoon. "I could probably make it up here in my sedan the way it looks right now. Sure is pretty coming down, though."

"Perfect night for putting up what will surely be the most perfect Christmas tree in all the land. Even if only a handful of people besides us will get to enjoy it."

Carol eyed the crowd of trees growing close and thick against the narrow road, reduced to dark smudges by the snow. From a couple of years of working for Miss Kellen, she knew the forest on this side of Maple Ridge was made up of oaks, poplars, and the typical abundance of maple trees.

This land wasn't part of the vast, thick ring of harvested sugar maples that gave the town its name and most of its livelihood. The original builders over a hundred and twenty years ago—working for a wealthy land, coal, and timber baron—knew the first Kellens to occupy the house would have never tolerated the shocking violation of their privacy caused by maple sap harvesting.

Otherwise they wouldn't have gone through the trouble of choosing such a remote, isolated location for their fabulous retreat back in the days when the treacherous road up the mountain was made of rocks and mud.

Carol had no trouble believing the stories of how they'd brought in oxen rather than horses for hauling up building materials they couldn't find right there.

But what worried her tonight was the bunches of pine trees. The first Mr. Kellen had insisted on having them planted all over for exactly this time of year.

The idea of his dear wife and children and grandchildren and beyond being subjected to an entirely gray and barren landscape all winter long was intolerable to him. So every species of tree and bush that held onto their leaves year-round became a permanent part of the landscape on the sprawling grounds at the high end of Maple Ridge.

"What's got you spooked?" Sid said. "You're watching the trees like something's going to jump out after us."

Carol shoved him with a playful elbow.

"It's not what might jump out of the trees. It's the trees themselves, especially the pines along this road. Some of those old ones are huge, you know? They'd be tough to clear if even one of them fell."

Sid looked more closely now, shaking his head.

Like most kids who grew up in Maple Ridge, they'd both spent time working either at the Maple Barn or out in the ring of trees that kept it supplied. Even outside of late winter harvest season, the job of tree maintenance never stopped.

Understanding what kept a tree healthy and in good shape was pretty much hardwired by the time they graduated high school.

"They've stood there a long time, haven't they?" he said. "Good thing it's not supposed to snow too much tonight."

Carol shrugged as she navigated down the long, straight driveway to the house itself. The snow collected more here than it had in town. Even a hundred feet in elevation once they were as high as Maple Ridge could make a huge difference.

Still, the dashboard thermometer read well above freezing.

"As far as I know," she said, "Miss Kellen just wants the tree decorated, so we shouldn't be out here too long. But you now how she is. Halfway through the main job, she'll think up fifty little jobs that she trusts to us and nobody else."

"And sneak in those bonuses she knows two aspiring college students can't resist. Every trip out here somehow turns into an adventure."

Carol mentally reviewed what she'd saved against the costs of the excellent college down in Hidden Springs. After years of working as much as they possibly could, she and Sid just about had enough to cover four years of expenses with only part-time jobs and no loans.

Miss Kellen's bonuses—and her support of local kids—was more than enough to make up for her eccentricity.

Like the porch at Sid's, the lights of the Kellen house were the first things to peek through the dancing veils of white.

Unlike Sid's house, there were easily a dozen lights in festive red, green, and blue, scattered across two broad, tall levels.

The house was hardly as stunning as the Biltmore in Asheville, North Carolina, but it was impressive by local standards. The wooden siding was currently painted a surprisingly warm shade of green—another contrast to the gloom of bare trees. A deep porch ran the length of the house, with a duplicate above it on the second floor.

Carol was relieved as always that Miss Kellen kept the Christmas lights for both porches in place year-round. At least she and Sid wouldn't be struggling to hang those tonight. Some poor handyman or electrician might have to scramble around and look for burned out bulbs or shorts later, but not tonight.

According to carefully followed tradition, no outdoor lights would be lit until the tree was properly decorated.

The house was nowhere near as ornate as the elaborate Victorians other wealthy folks had built back then. The Kellens once owned one down in Hidden Springs that was rumored to have been the most extravagantly carved and painted for miles around.

For this retreat, they'd gone simple. Solid.

And probably most importantly out in the middle of nowhere, easy to maintain.

Carol parked in front of the wide matching garage originally built to shelter horse carriages. The adjoining barn for the horses was long gone. She and Sid would be wrangling crates of decorations stored out there rather than any sort of equine maintenance.

Thankfully a covered walkway between the garage and the house would shelter them from having to repeatedly tromp through the open.

Two sets of tire tracks rapidly filling in with snow showed someone else had recently arrived and tucked into the third section of the garage, furthest from the house. Miss Kellen always kept her sports car and her sensible sedan in the middle garage. The live-in housekeeper was the only other person who usually parked in the garages.

"Wonder who's up here for the festivities?" Sid said, zipping his coat. "Usually what's left of the family doesn't show up until the Solstice party, after Miss Kellen and the rest of us have done all the work."

"I've always wondered why none of the rest of her family live here with her. Not a word about them, besides the rumor that one of the cousins is constantly fussing and threatening to sue. Miss Kellen lived away until about ten years ago, I think, but the house and everything inside belongs to her."

She reached up and turned his face toward her, then gave him a good kiss right on the lips, getting a sweet smile in return.

"Hey, the more the merrier, right?" she said. "Maybe they'll actually help us with all those garlands and a hundred strings of lights on this year's gigantic tree."

The lovely scent of a wood fire filled the air as soon as she opened the door. Sid laughed, and the thick-falling snow deadened the sound, making Carol's ears feel like they were stuffed full of cotton.

"You know the time-honored town gossip as well as I do," he said. "No unexpected visit from a Kellen has ever been good news. Not since..."

"Great-great-great Uncle Christopher surprised that generation's Mr. Kellen," Carol picked up, adopting the low voice required for such a scandalous—and tragic—event in Maple Ridge history. "And no one found the body until the spring thaw."

They stepped up on the porch, careful to stomp and brush off the snowflakes so they wouldn't melt all over something either antique, valuable, or at least beloved inside. Several vigorous scoots on dark brown bristly mats took care of stray moisture or mud on their shoes.

Sid nodded gravely as Carol stepped up to the gleaming oak door already hung with a gigantic holly and ivy wreath studded with dried cranberries.

"And as long as everyone remembers to never, ever show up by surprise, all will be well." He winked and pushed the doorbell's glowing blue button. "Assuming that was the *only* body to be found."

The speculation among kids and adults alike who worked for Miss Kellen—that she hovered close by when they were expected to arrive—renewed itself when she opened the door a quick second later.

Carol was always surprised by how *young* Miss Kellen looked.

She had to be in her late thirties, maybe early forties, but her heart-shaped face was curiously unlined. She wore blue jeans like Carol and Sid, though her purple button-up work shirt looked brand new. Miss Kellen's red hair was pulled away from her face, probably into the usual thick braid down her back.

Her welcoming smile made her look closer to Carol's age.

"So *good* to see you, come in out of the cold." Miss Kellen waved them inside, then closed the door. "Thank you for making the trip on a day like this."

"You're welcome, Miss Kellen," Sid said. "Always happy to help out when we can."

Miss Kellen clasped her hands together in front of her chest. Her cheeks were a bit more flushed than usual.

"Let me show you the tree so you'll get an idea what we're up against. Then we'll get started."

She spun on her heel and charged out of the small entry hall, leaving Carol and Sid to slip off their coats and hang them on a row of jet-black hooks. Carol kept her hat on to avoid both hair frizz and frozen ears when they had to go back out.

The old-fashioned plaster-and-lath walls in the entry were newly painted a rich gold, a wonderful counterpoint to the dark hardwood floor that featured in every room of the house.

Like every other scrap of wood and a good bit of the stone, the flooring was said to have come from right here on the mountain. Even what they could see of the gorgeous staircase opposite the way Miss Kellen went—leading to the mysterious upstairs and darkness—had been pieced together with leftovers from construction.

When Carol followed Miss Kellen into the huge sitting room, she nearly stopped in her tracks. Only knowing Sid was right behind and more likely to crash into her than stop kept her moving.

The room's overwhelming variety of sofas, chairs, and ottomans—all modern but in neutral shades so they'd blend in—normally faded into the background beside bunches of paintings and photographs on the walls. From brand new nature and travel photos surrounded by minimalist black metal back to family portraits from Kellen ancestors framed in elaborate carved wood, Miss Kellen somehow made them all work together.

It was hard to say the same of several built-in shelves and antique tables loaded down with strange memorabilia.

Ancient china clocks, books from every era, metal and glass sculptures, too many knives to count. Weird travel souvenirs like salt and pepper shakers from all over the world, some of them old-fashioned and insensitive enough to be downright shocking to Carol's eye.

A few items stored under glass domes she suspected were bones, but was too afraid to ask.

The bizarre collection spilled over to the wide mantel over a roaring fire.

As the Kellen's fortunes declined, everyone from the extended family dumped their portable treasure up here, which was probably the disaffected cousin's justification for threatened lawsuits and complaining. Hardly anyone who wasn't one of the housekeepers (always hired from out of town) had seen more than a couple of the rooms.

After a sharp financial hit in the Seventies and Eighties, the family itself seemed to decline as much as their wealth. Now hardly any of them were left besides Miss Kellen, rattling around in this huge old house by herself most of the time. Even her occasional *special* friends never seemed to stay long, or spend much time out in Maple Ridge.

Tonight, Carol couldn't drag her eyes away from the strangest Christmas tree she'd ever seen, standing in front of a huge picture window facing toward the back yard.

Taller than Sid, the fir tree was wide enough to be two trees, maybe three. The branches were covered with thick bunches of dark green needles that had a peculiar yellowish tint. A strong, spicy fir smell brought a rather aggressive bite to the air.

Miss Kellen stood beside the odd tree, her hands clasped just below her chin this time.

"Well? What do you think?"

Carol recovered her voice first.

"It's just beautiful, Miss Kellen. I've never seen that kind of tree before."

Miss Kellen grinned and reached out to run her hand along one of the branches.

"Oh good," she said, her voice a bit too loud and her words too fast. "I wanted something different this year. Not the same old Douglas fir or scotch pine."

"What kind of tree is it?" Sid said, with an impressive look of curiosity rather than the startlement Carol felt.

She was afraid if she asked herself, she'd sound like someone trying (and failing) to compliment a relative's baby who was anything but cute.

"It's a *grand* fir," Miss Kellen said reverently, before her words sped up even more. "I think that name suits it perfectly, don't you? And this one is even more special. It started out as an accident, really, tucked away at the end of the row where no one was paying attention. Someone planted two seedlings too close together, so they grew together into one trunk, but two tops. Someone would have yanked it out of the ground if they'd been paying attention. It gives us so much more room for decorating."

Carol nodded, focusing on the tree. She was afraid if she looked at Sid, they'd both start laughing.

"We'd better get started, then," she said. "Just in case that snow does pick up later."

Miss Kellen beamed. "Everything is out in the first garage, along with all the extra decorations I bought. I even sent for one of those little hand trucks so it won't be so hard to bring everything inside. I had to bring in a few new things to go along with the new tree."

"I can't wait to see everything," Carol lied through her teeth. The quick tree decorating trip had magically gotten longer, just as she expected.

It was on the tip of her tongue to ask about those extra tire tracks heading into the garage, but she decided not to.

Just get in, get this finished, and get away so she and Sid could compare notes.

"We'll bring the first load in so we can get started," Sid said.

"Wonderful!" Miss Kellen exclaimed loudly enough that Carol jumped. Miss Kellen dropped the black plastic square of the garage door opener into Sid's hand. "I'll make sure everything is ready for hot chocolate after."

As soon as Carol closed the front door behind them, Sid stared at her with wide eyes.

"Wow," he said. "Where did she get that thing?"

"And how did she get it shipped all the way out here? I've never even *heard* of a tree like that, much less a mutant double version."

They walked the length of the porch toward the garage, doing their best to keep the giggling to a reasonable level. A quick trot along the covered path, paved to match the driveway, and Sid used the garage door opener to send the wood-paneled door rolling upward.

"I hope she didn't get too much," Sid said. "I don't like the looks of that snow now."

Carol looked down the driveway. The snow still

floated down in huge flakes, and rather than collecting on the pavement, it still melted almost as fast as it fell.

Then she caught sight of a lacy, delicate evergreen bush close to the porch. It was nearly flattened with a growing load of the wet snow.

"I see what you mean," she said. "A dusting on the road won't mean much if a couple of those old pines really do come down. Let's get moving."

An automatic light revealed an extremely neat space large enough to park two cars, the ancient pebbly concrete always swept clean. This closest garage—walled off all around like the others—was given over entirely to storage. Deep wooden shelves lined the walls, all of them full of carefully organized and labeled crates and boxes.

Four huge cardboard boxes marked *Christmas* in precise writing waited in their usual spot. Against the back wall, second shelf, right in the middle.

In the center of the normally clear floor sat two huge Amazon boxes displaying the trademark smile, with a modest black hand truck leaned against them. The upright handles didn't look overly sturdy, but the platform at the bottom was wide enough to hold the largest box.

"I suppose two new boxes is reasonable for such a...generous tree," Carol said, walking forward to tip one of the boxes back. "Not very heavy at all, just awkward as hell."

Sid stood beside her, hands on his hips.

"You'd think whoever brought all of this could have taken the stuff into the house. I wouldn't mind pretty much any other night."

Carol helped him move the new boxes onto the hand truck, then added one of the older ones from the shelf. Only a couple of those were heavy. The rest were packed full of garlands and pillows and carefully rolled up strings of lights. Again, awkward, but manageable.

They secured the load with several bungee cords from an absurdly orderly collection of them hanging from the wall beside the door. Still, she walked beside Sid to steady the load.

"I don't see any footprints, do you?" she said, glancing back over her shoulder.

The garage had enough of an overhang that whoever drove up earlier could have avoided leaving prints if they were careful. But she and Sid had left several on the way out, and each of them stepped into the snow boundary now.

"The tire tracks are almost gone. Maybe they have tiny feet?"

That set Carol off laughing again, at the image of

a regular-sized person mincing along on feet a few inches long.

"That or it was a ghost," she said. "Maybe Great-great-great Uncle Christopher come back for revenge."

Carol's mood shifted as they rolled along the pathway and across the porch. What she thought of as her superstitious side crept back in around her edges.

"Miss Kellen *is* acting a little strange," she whispered. "Her face is red and she seems kind of...manic, I guess? And where is the housekeeper? Gosh, Katie's been here since at least Easter. That might be a record."

"I wondered if Miss Kellen had too much coffee today myself." He winked at her. "Think it's one of her extra-special friends, stopped by for a quick one before the Solstice party?"

Carol smiled as they reached the door.

Of course. That would explain Miss Kellen's jumpiness and Katie not being around tonight.

"That makes a lot more sense than the crazy stuff I've been thinking. I'm not sure why she thinks *we'd* mind, though. She knows we've been dating since we were in high school. I corrupted what little virtue you had years ago."

Before Sid could answer, Miss Kellen yanked the

front door open so hard the wreath swung and thumped back into place. Her cheeks were still bright red, but at least she wasn't near-shouting now.

"Oh good, the hand truck is working. I was afraid it would be too small. Let's get everything inside."

Two more trips got the other boxes, and each time, Carol was more tempted to wander down to the third garage to have a peek. Or at least to see if there were footprints. And still no sign of another person inside the house.

When they walked in from the final trip, Miss Kellen was kneeling on the floor beside one of the open Amazon boxes, giggling like a school kid. Her words again stumbled over each other on the way out.

"These lights are simply gorgeous, don't you think? They'll look like tiny little meteors falling in every color." She put the bundle of long, narrow lights back in the box and pulled out a what looked like a rolled net covered with dots. "And these will hang along the hallways. It will be like walking through a gorgeous fairy land waterfall!"

Carol finally pulled her toboggan off and shoved it into her back pocket, no longer worried about how fuzzy her hair might look. Miss Kellen had always been friendly and encouraging, but she'd never used such...fanciful language.

Carol was also a lot less worried about being inappropriate with her employer after hearing the bizarre way she was talking.

"You doing okay, Miss Kellen?"

Miss Kellen looked up so fast her red braid flipped over her shoulder. She didn't seem offended or angry.

Only a little bit...frightened.

"Whatever do you mean, Carol?"

Without so much as a blink, all the lights went out.

Miss Kellen let out a little-girl cry so heart-breaking that Carol put a hand on her shoulder. The glow from the fireplace was bright enough to show how big and worried Sid's eyes were.

"Hang on, I'll grab a flashlight," he said, pulling out his phone and thumbing the light on. "I don't think I've ever had reason to ask, but do you have a generator up here, Miss Kellen?"

Miss Kellen covered her mouth with one hand, but she nodded slowly. She then grabbed her braid with both hands, running her fingers along the length. Carol had to force herself not to try to still that restless motion.

"There is one, yes," Miss Kellen said, staring into the fireplace. She wasn't as loud, but her words still tumbled out in a rush. "Don't you worry about that,

Sid. I've got plenty of candles and firewood here. I'm sure the power company will be up here in no time to get everything back up and running. We'll have to schedule the tree decorating another time, so you can both go on back home now."

Sid turned a look of mild panic toward Carol.

"Hang on, I can sure help you get the generator going," he said. "Just let me know where it is."

Carol nodded, moving until she was between Miss Kellen and the fire.

Miss Kellen, who had a strange combination of fear and blankness on her face that creeped Carol out terribly.

"And I'll call the power company right now," Carol said. "So we can get them on the way while Sid gets your generator going."

Pulling her own phone out, Carol tried to do an internet search for the number. After a second of watching it attempt to connect, she realized the signal was too weak to get online.

She'd never thought twice about getting on the WiFi here, and she'd heard Miss Kellen mention something about a cellular booster. Neither of which were apparently on any kind of emergency backup circuit.

"Do you have a phone book I can use?" Carol

said, trying to remember when she'd last even seen one.

Miss Kellen shook her head, but not hard enough to pull her braid out of her hands.

"I have one, in the kitchen. But the power company's number is written on the board beside the house phone. That won't matter, though, not now."

She took a deep breath, squared her shoulders, and placed her hands flat on her thighs.

"If that was a tree that made the power go out," she went on, "it would have taken the phone line, too. That's all buried in the yard, close to the house, of course. But down at the end of the road, those lines run together. The power company wouldn't bury those."

"I'll check the phone," Sid said, heading toward the kitchen. "Why don't you tell Carol where the generator is? She knows how to start one up, too."

Carol knelt in front of Miss Kellen, shifting until she blocked the view of the fire.

"How about that generator, Miss Kellen?"

"Oh, it's outside the kitchen, under a little overhang so it won't get wet. But it doesn't have gas. I have it serviced and emptied out every spring. That's best for generators, instead of letting them sit all summer long when you don't need them."

Carol took her own deep breath, so she wouldn't

snap or yell. She wanted to shake Miss Kellen's shoulders to get her to concentrate. Yes, losing her job was reason enough *not* to on its own.

Making every effort not to further upset a woman who was in some kind of distress multiplied her need for patience greatly.

"So you probably have gas here too, right? Or maybe a chainsaw, in case the road is blocked. I can drive you into town. There's no need to stay up here all by yourself, Miss Kellen."

All the hairs on Carol's arms tried to stand up when Miss Kellen locked gazes with her.

The vague expression of fear had intensified until it felt like a clammy hand touching the back of her neck.

"The phone *is* out," Sid said just then, walking back out from the kitchen with a huge yellow flashlight in his hand. "I can't get enough signal to make a call, either. Let's all just load up and head into town, assuming we can get past if trees are down. Hey, do you happen to have a chainsaw?"

"We need to let our parents know what's going on, too," Carol said, not looking at Sid. "You don't have to do anything. You can stay right here by the fire. We'll take care of it all."

Carol froze, realization tearing through her. She

leaned closer and touched Miss Kellen's shoulder again, then spoke in a low voice.

"All that stuff, the chainsaw, the gas. That's in the third garage, isn't it? I saw the tire tracks when we got here. You don't want us to go out there."

Miss Kellen covered Carol's hand with her own, and despite the warm fire her hand was colder than the snow.

"You *can't* go out there, Carol. It's not safe for anyone."

Carol saw Sid ease toward the front door out of the corner of her eye, somehow moving without making a sound despite his lanky build and big feet. She willed him to grab something in case it really was dangerous, maybe the axe from beside the covered woodpile behind the garages.

She didn't dare look away from Miss Kellen's terrified eyes.

"Tell me why it's not safe. Is someone else here now? Or maybe earlier today?"

Miss Kellen shook her head several times, the movement as fast and jerky as her speech.

"No no, no one out there. No one at all. If we just stay here, stay inside, the power company will figure it out and come get us. Or the phone company will, they'll be sure to notice."

"Who made the tire tracks?" Carol said, ignoring

the voice in her head telling her she shouldn't ask such questions. "If they're not here now, why are you so upset?"

Carol jumped at a creaking noise from right over her head, but she forced herself not to look away from Miss Kellen.

Who didn't move or react at all.

"No one else is here," Miss Kellen said in a high voice, with a smile that got too big in a hurry. "Everything is perfectly fine."

"So you won't mind a bit if I go upstairs and see what that noise was?"

Miss Kellen closed her eyes, and her smile stretched into a rictus.

"I would mind, yes. But I don't think I'd be able to stop you. Or Sid."

Carol started to get up and go do just that, but her flesh crawled at the idea of walking up the stairs she'd never climbed, then trying to find her way around when she had no clue where the rooms were up there. All that on top of the power being out.

Visions of some variety of dangerous criminal hiding out up there rather than a secret lover made the idea even less appealing.

She decided to take a chance instead.

"Sid can't go upstairs right now, Miss Kellen. He

just went out to check the third garage to see if he could find that chainsaw."

Miss Kellen's eyes opened wide and she lurched to her feet, knocking against Carol hard enough to throw her sideways onto her hip and one hand.

"He can't go out there! We have to stop him, Carol, help me!"

She grabbed Carol's arm and tugged. After resisting for a second, Carol let Miss Kellen pull her upright. If nothing else to keep her shoulder un-dislocated.

"He's already out there, but we can help him. Tell me why, Miss Kellen!"

She dragged Carol several steps toward the front door, shaking her head the whole way.

"It wasn't Katie's fault," she said, now sounding angry instead of afraid. "She *never* should have come up here in the first place, certainly not without letting me know. Now it's all going to fall apart and cause ever so much trouble."

Carol braced herself against the door to the entryway with one hand, hoping Miss Kellen would stop pulling her arm before it actually did hurt.

"Katie? Isn't she out of town?"

Carol nearly screamed when a voice floated down the darkened stairway.

"I'm right here."

Miss Kellen turned that way and covered her mouth, still shaking her head.

Katie didn't look any different than she usually did as she walked down. Khaki pants, sky blue golf shirt, brown hair pulled in a ponytail. Her face was overly pale, even for wintertime, and she gripped the stair rail tight. As if she was injured, or maybe trying to cover shaking hands.

Carol said "Are you okay, Katie?" at the same time Miss Kellen repeated it wasn't Katie's fault.

All at once, the ghosts of Kellen misfortune felt thick and heavy in the air.

Especially the sad fate of Great-great-great Uncle Christopher.

Carol couldn't stop herself from shivering, and sincerely wishing the damn phones weren't out.

"I certainly have been *better*," Katie said, her voice rising as she waved her free hand. "I know you wanted me to stay upstairs and out of sight, Miss Kellen, but I felt awful letting all of you bumble around in the dark like that."

All three women jumped when Sid shoved the front door open much too hard. Carol caught it before it could knock Miss Kellen in the head.

"Carol?" he said, reaching for her hand. "You better..." His gaze darted to Miss Kellen, then Katie. "Maybe we should all go out to the garage.

Together. Yeah, that would be best. Then...I don't know."

Miss Kellen hugged herself and took a step back, but Katie only nodded as she took the last step and joined them in the crowded entry.

"We may as well," she said. "It's not like there's anything more to hide now."

Sid pulled Carol closer to him and put his arm around her.

"I don't want to know what else could be hidden around here," he said. "Except maybe the gas for the generator."

Katie stared at him for a second, then let out a bark of laughter.

"I think I can handle that much." She took Miss Kellen by the arm. "Come on, Sandra. You don't have to look again, but I don't think it's a good idea for you to stay in here by yourself. It's been a hard enough day for you already. Me too."

Carol fought a surprisingly strong urge to refuse to go outside, to never have to find out what was making the others act so weird.

Her normal default in life was to find out the truth, then deal with how it made her feel.

She was afraid keeping herself in the dark, so to speak, would make more sense in this case.

But she reached for her coat, then watched Katie

pull out her own pink jacket and Miss Kellen's forest green wool coat out of the closet. Sid was so shaken that Carol had to help him with his.

Back outside against her better judgement, Carol was briefly relieved by the state of the driveway. Huge flakes still floated down, and the grass was completely covered by a few inches of snow that glittered white under Sid's flashlight. The bush close to the house was entirely flattened under the heavy, wet layer, barely visible now.

Thank goodness the driveway was still melting the snow almost as fast as it collected. Only a light coating had caught on. If the temperature dropped fast overnight, black ice could be a real worry.

But for now, she was a hell of a lot more worried about whatever they were walking toward. The fresh, crackling cold air and whispery sound surrounding them, normally her favorite parts of snowfall, faded into the background.

The third garage door stood open, with several little drifts of snow well past the line left by the overhanging roof. Probably pulled inside when Sid had to heave the door open with the power out.

Carol glanced back at Katie and Miss Kellen in the light from Sid's amazingly bright flashlight, trying not to let her overactive imagination get away with her. The two women were not, in fact, sneaking over to Carol's Jeep to make their escape and leave her and Sid stranded. Neither were they creeping ever closer with assorted bludgeoning devices in hand.

The truth was Miss Kellen held on to Katie's arm with both hands, and both of them stared straight ahead.

Not exactly normal or reassuring, no. But not life-threatening.

When she stepped around the corner and looked inside, Carol grabbed Sid's arm, trying not to hold too tight.

The garage didn't have shelves all around like the first one, only gardening and yardwork supplies against the back wall. Including tools for trimming and even cutting trees, like two of the chainsaws Sid was looking for, and more than one axe. All hanging neatly on the wall, but with a few empty spots clustered together.

Plenty of room for the silver pickup truck parked inside. Now that she saw it, Carol recognized it as Katie's: often used for bringing in groceries, packages, and supplies.

A black sedan she'd never seen before was parked inside, too. An older model but expensive, with license plates from a few hours away in North Carolina.

It was the dark stain on the otherwise spotless concrete floor that captured all of Carol's attention.

The body in front of the truck captured all the air in her lungs.

"Anyone want to tell me what's going on?" Sid said, his voice not nearly as shaky as Carol felt. "Or maybe start with who that is?"

"That's Monica Kellen," Katie said. Her face was nearly the same shade as the snow. "Or it was. Miss Kellen's cousin."

Miss Kellen only stared into the garage with a slight frown on her face.

"But what *happened*?" Carol managed to say.

"Well, I was coming back from Wolf Branch," Katie said. "Picking up supplies for the party. I knew the two of you were coming up, so I was in a hurry to get back and help. When I saw that car in the garage where it wasn't supposed to be, I guess I got...distracted. I never saw her until it was too late."

Miss Kellen shook herself and stood to the side, hands on her hips. The hectic red was back in her cheeks. She spoke quickly, but now without the sense of her words chasing each other out of her mouth.

"That's *not* what you said, Katie, when you were still too upset to think up a way to make it all your fault. You told me Monica darted out right in front of you, and I believe it. She probably didn't expect you to be here. I think if you hadn't come back when you did, she would have either broken into the house tonight or at least tried to stir up some kind of trouble again."

"Again?" Carol said, her voice not much more than a squeak.

Miss Kellen crossed her arms, her features shifting into a scowl.

"Monica drove up here three times over the last few months, even after I asked her not to. It might sound silly, but the whole family *does* try to avoid showing up here unannounced. We grew up with that dreadful story just like everyone else in Maple Ridge. Monica always seemed to know when Katie would be out, and no one else would be here working or visiting."

"I still think she was tapping your phone," Katie said, rubbing her hands together. "Or hacking your email."

"That may be," Miss Kellen said. "I wouldn't be surprised. I let her in the first time, and she said the most awful things to me. Yelling and carrying on, threatening me with legal action and physical harm. Accusing me of stealing some kind of valuable paintings I honestly have never seen in my life. The only stealing that happened between us was when she took one of the garage door openers that day."

She paused, and Carol was startled to see tears running down her cheeks.

"I don't know what got into her, I truly don't. The next time she parked right inside the garage, probably to show me she could, and I refused to let her in. She screamed and pounded on the door for an hour before she gave up and left. The last time, I finally called the rest of the family and told them what was happening. I'd so hoped they could talk some sense into her. A couple of them thought they did."

She crossed her arms tightly across her chest, then let her breath out in a cloud of vapor in the falling snow.

"I know they'd all agreed she wasn't welcome for the party, not that I care one whit about that anymore. Someone *must* have told her. And now...this."

"I'm sorry, Miss Kellen," Sid said. "But I think we have to call the police now. Or whenever we can get out of here."

Miss Kellen squeezed her eyes closed and clenched her fists. Katie took her arm and walked them just under the roof and out of the snow. Carol wanted very much to resist when Sid did the same with his arm around her shoulders.

She went anyway, heart pounding and stomach

flip-flopping, standing where the truck blocked her view of Monica Kellen. And the tools that had fallen with her.

Carol refused to go an inch further.

"I wanted to call earlier," Katie said softly. "But she begged me not to. She said we had to figure out what to do first."

"Is it any wonder I got upset? They're going to think *I* killed her," Miss Kellen said, her voice tight. Her eyes blazed at Carol, then Sid. "The whole family knows about her sneaking up here and how upset I was. How scared. That or the police will accuse *you*, Katie."

"Is it too much to hope you have some kind of security camera out here?" Carol said.

Katie looked up with a sad half-smile.

"I put in an order to have them installed. No one could get here until after the new year."

"Okay, we have to get this sorted out," Sid said. "Have either of you touched...the body?"

Katie and Miss Kellen shook their heads. Inside Carol marveled at having to convince someone to call the sheriff with a dead body in their garage, but she suspected trying to make that point by getting upset and yelling wouldn't work.

"Then everything will turn out okay," she said. "Let's do what Sid suggested and try to get to town.

We'll have to at least get back to the road to get signal, right? We'll just have to...have to get..."

Katie scowled for a second, then set her mouth in a firm line.

"I'll get them."

She patted Miss Kellen's shoulder, then walked into the garage, going around the black sedan, away from the body. She picked up the smaller of the two chainsaws. Before she turned to come back out, Sid squared his shoulders and went in after the big one.

Carol stepped closer to Miss Kellen, wishing she had the courage to hug her.

"It's going to be okay, Miss Kellen."

Carol had to fight back tears of her own at the way Miss Kellen stared at her for a second, then all the tension seemed to leave her face and shoulders and her whole body at once. Instead of worrying about appropriate behavior or what anyone else in town or on the whole planet might think, Carol caught Miss Kellen up in a hug after all.

Both of them wiped their cheeks as they stepped back.

"After all this, Carol, I think it makes more sense for you and Sid to call me Sandra."

IN THE END, they only needed the chainsaws for one of the pine trees.

Several were indeed down, unable to carry the weight of the heavy snow after days of warm rain had loosened their hold on the soil. Thankfully none of the real giants were among the fallen. Either the four of them pushing or Carol's Jeep and the chains she kept in back for emergencies handled most of the trees with no trouble at all.

At the end of the driveway, they ran into one that wedged itself too hard into the trees across the road to shift without cutting it up.

While Carol, Sid, and Katie worked on the tree, Miss Kellen walked alone through the gorgeous still-falling snow, to the main road to call the sheriff down in Wolf Branch.

She returned looking sad but determined, and carried as much of the branches and wood off to the side as everyone else without saying a word.

When they all piled back into the Jeep, breathing hard and bringing the sharp aroma of fresh-cut pine, she finally spoke.

"I asked the sheriff to meet us at your house, Carol, I hope that's okay. They'll bring me and Katie back out here. For the investigation."

"We'll do anything we can to help," Sid said from the back seat beside Katie.

Miss Kellen—Sandra—turned to look at all of them with a shy smile.

"Just by being here for me tonight you've all done plenty. I wouldn't think of having the usual Solstice party now, but I hope you'll all join me for one later on once all this awfulness settles down. Your families, too, to breathe a little life into the old house. Maybe in the new year."

Carol looked into Sid's eyes and smiled. He'd been right on the way out here, what felt like years ago.

The trip had definitely turned into an adventure.

"That sounds good to me, Sandra," Carol said, putting the Jeep in gear and heading toward home.

JASON A. ADAMS

Author of *Angel of Mercy* and *Moulin Rouge*

THE NUMBER ONE KILLER

For all the puzzle solvers.

THE NUMBER ONE KILLER

S uch a beautiful day for such a tragic scene.

Dr. Maureen Fitzgerald, spending her first year of residency in rural medicine, stood with her mentor on the redwood deck of a beige doublewide mobile home with unmoving mint-green faux shutters. The home sat tucked back on a tiny patch of flat land halfway up Snowball Hollow and all the way at the end of the road.

Snowball *Holler*, she reminded herself. She still got weird looks from the locals if she pronounced certain words the way they were spelled.

The bright September sunshine lit up a mountainside full of vivid fall colors. Bloody maple trees, golden oaks, bright yellow tulip poplars. The deep green of rhododendron and mountain laurel in the understory made the whole hill look like Paul Bunyan's flower garden.

She loved the smells of autumn. The furry organic scent of damp leaves mixed with the homey aromas of wood or coal smoke from nearly every chimney.

Much better than the noticeable, but not quite turned, odor of two-day-old death.

The weather had been up and down like a yo-yo so far this fall, but today was mild enough that she could wear her UVA t-shirt, with the green plaid flannel that Dr. Emerson had given her tied around her waist. She might need the flannel, or something thicker if the wind changed direction and came roaring down the hollow instead of going across the ridgetops with the sound of a jet engine.

Holler.

"You need to be ready for anything in this job," Doc Em had told her. "'Specially when it comes to the weather. Nothin' worse than trying to do all this doctor stuff with numb fingers."

"The Job" in this case was County Medical Examiner. Mo's dad wanted her to follow him into the Neurology Department at Duke, but she was fascinated by the puzzle of death. Its causes and clues. What she could learn from what autopsy could tell her.

In the remote coalfields of far Southwest Virginia, that wasn't much.

Most people here died of simple things.

Car crashes. Overdose. Pulmonary disease and myocardial infarctions. Plain old age.

But not Jerry Gardner. At least, nothing pointed that direction.

Yet.

Deputy Betty Stanley was in the mobile home's living room, holding the vic's hysterically sobbing wife, rocking her gently. Betty knew the family well, like most folks in this sparsely settled corner of the coalfields.

Mo had been here nearly two months, doing the intern thing. Doc Em was a great mentor. She supposed she should call him her attending, but she liked mentor better.

Doc Em was a sixty-three-year-old African-American with cotton-ball gray hair over a face as dark as the coal that had been this area's lifeblood for generations. Instead of the usual white coat, he wore a blue padded jacket, brown corduroy trousers, and a houndstooth driving cap.

His face held very few lines, except for those at the corners of his eyes and around his mouth that grew a little deeper with each of his many smiles. He was full-time country doctor and as-needed ME for the three adjacent counties.

He was a local, but had done med school down in Atlanta at Morehouse, done his residency at Grady Memorial. His skill at treating victims of gang warfare made him one of the best at treating hunting accidents and blunt force trauma. It also made him a damn fine ME when the cops needed info on the few suspected homicides that came in.

Which is why he'd brought her up in this *holler* today.

Ellen Gardner had returned home at approximately ten-fifteen that morning. She'd been in Pikeville, Kentucky, spending a few days with her ailing aunt. She'd returned after no one had been able to reach her husband by phone for two days, discovered the body lying on the kitchen floor, and called 911 immediately.

Preliminary investigation by the sheriff's office showed no signs of forced entry, and Ida Mullins down at the foot of the road didn't recall anyone driving up toward the Gardner residence until Mrs. Gardner's return.

No obvious signs of injury on the body. Nothing obvious missing. Vic still had his wallet, truck keys still in the dish by the door.

Jerry Gardener was thirty-six years old. Didn't smoke, didn't dip chaw, didn't drink to excess. No known enemies. No history of major medical issues that Doc Em could recall, and he'd been the vic's doctor since boyhood.

Sheriff Doyle and an investigator Mo didn't know by name yet came out from the kitchen, stripping off latex gloves.

"All yours, Doc," the sheriff said. "Not lookin' like a murder investigation, but I'd sure appreciate you tellin' me what might'a killed that boy."

"We'll see what there is to see, Tom. Dr. Fitzgerald, if you would accompany me?"

Mo pulled on her own gloves, then picked up her notebook, turned on the digital VOX recorder in her pocket, and clipped the tiny mike to her collar. Checked her watch.

"Preliminary in situ examination of deceased, Gerald Arthur Gardner, conducted by Dr. Abraham Emerson. Dr. Maureen Fitzgerald assisting." She added the time and date as they moved into the kitchen.

Cheery harvest gold linoleum and the red-checked tablecloth contrasted sharply with the body on the floor. The breeze coming in through the open window over the sink fluttered a set of curtains with a cute purple paisley print. Through the window, she saw tree trunks and bushes only a few yards away, rising up the hillside.

She blocked everything else out but the job she was here to do.

Knelt beside the body. Focused.

"Deceased is in left lateral decubitus position. A chair is nearby and overturned, possibly the deceased fell from chair."

"You're doing good, Mo," Doc Em said, leaning casually against the counter. "What can you tell me about the body?"

She checked flexibility of his arms and legs. Carefully lifted the blue chambray workshirt and examined the skin tone. No need to check temperature, not with the rigor and livor bruising where the body met on the floor.

"Rigor mortis is present, but beginning to dissipate. Livor mortis pattern indicates the deceased has not been moved since TOD, which would on first approximation have occurred between thirty-six and forty-eight hours ago. Last known contact with deceased was by the spouse, approximately ten p.m. three days ago. No visible external trauma, although full examination will be conducted at the Lonesome Pine Medical Center once the deceased can be transported."

"Nothin' to see here," Doc Em said. "Turn that fancy tape recorder off and come walk with me."

Mo stood, clicking the recorder off. "Walk? Where?"

"So far as you, I, and Tom—Sheriff Doyle, that is—can see, ain't no good reason this boy ought to be lyin' there. So, we take him back to the morgue and cut him up, lookin' for anything might be out of true, right?"

"Yeah, I mean what else?"

"Let's take a peek around the place. Might see somethin' that can guide our investigation. Besides, it sure is a nice day."

They walked back outside, past the deputies and Mrs. Gardner. She was still crying, but softly now. Talking in a low voice with Betty, who still held one of her hands.

A good reminder for Mo. She loved solving the puzzle of death, but it was good to keep firmly in her mind that the deceased wasn't the only one affected.

Outside, Doc Em pointed to a white plastic disc nailed to one of the deck rails. A thermometer. The needle sat between sixty and seventy.

"You recall what the temperature was day before yesterday?" he asked.

"Um, around seventy, I think. That was the high,

anyway. Maybe sixty-two for the low. Comfortable weather, anyhow."

He didn't say anything else, just stuck his hands in his pockets, whistling as he ambled off the deck and around the side of the house. Mo trotted to catch up, wondering what he was looking for.

"Watch your feet," he said as she came around the house into the narrow strip of back yard. "Couple o' dead birds 'bout hid in the grass."

Mo saw the birds, a robin and a blue jay, their poor feet pointing at the sky. This house was not a happy place at all today.

When she looked up again, she saw Doc Em staring up the hill. She followed his gaze, saw a gate made of what looked like pipes welded together over a six or seven-foot-wide hole in the mountain.

"What's that, Doc?" she said, shading her eyes. "A cave?"

"I'd say it's a house pit. Scratch mine for furnace and stove coal. Bunch of those around here, but mostly blocked up these days. Too dangerous, and the big companies are just about giving coal away."

The wind shifted, rolling down the mountain, shaking a few vibrant leaves loose from the trees.

Doc Em took Mo's arm, began guiding her briskly back the way they'd come. "Best we get back around the house, make sure poor Jerry's loaded in the ambulance and ready to go, then get ourselves after him. We can start the autopsy after lunch. You mind takin' the knife on this one?"

He was going to let *her* do the autopsy? Hot damn! She couldn't help but grin, made sure her grin wasn't visible from the house.

"You're on, Doc. And lunch is on me."

THREE HOURS LATER, Mo shut off the morgue's overhead microphone, pulled off the heavy autopsy gloves, and rubbed her tired eyes.

"I don't get it, Doc. There's nothing here. Blood tox is negative. No bruising or laceration. Heart and lungs look good. This guy should be up and walking around, not lying on a slab."

Doc Em sat in his black vinyl wheelie chair, slowly turning himself from side to side, staring up at the ceiling and rubbing his chin.

"You consider asphyxia?" he said.

"No way. The window was open. I checked with Betty, and she said Mrs. Gardner didn't open it herself. Besides, like I said there's nothing in his blood."

"There wouldn't be, not if it was simple suffocation instead of chemical."

He spun some more, muttered to himself. Pulled his smartphone out and started tapping the screen.

"Big low pressure system moved through day before yesterday. That's interesting."

He put the phone back in his pocket. Turned back and forth, back and forth.

"I ever tell you my daddy mined coal? Worked his fingers to nubbins to help me get enough schoolin' not to follow in his footsteps."

Mo stayed quiet. Doc Em definitely had his thinking cap on.

"Do me a favor, Mo," he finally said as he stopped rotating. "Call up the Mine Safety and Health office over in Bristol. Find out if there's been any fracking activity in our area in the last couple of weeks."

"Huh?" Mo figured Doc Em probably knew what he was doing, but *she* sure had no clue. "Why? What would that mean?"

"Humor an old fart, sugar. I'll let you in once we hear what all they got to say."

Back at UVA and pretty much anywhere else, she'd have read the riot act to any male colleague who called her "sugar," but Doc Em she'd let get away with it. She got out the blue pages, marveling at how local governments could hang on to obsolete methods like phone books. Found the number, called. She explained who she was and why she was calling.

"You were right, Doc," she said as she disconnected. "One of the local natural gas companies has been fracking less than two miles from the Gardner place. How'd you know?"

"Oh, I didn't *know*. I just had a hunch. Don't let anyone tell you different, sometimes a hunch is an ME's best friend."

"I don't—" she began, but he held up a hand to stop her.

"Here's more hunch, honeybunch," he said, grinning. "Old coal mine above the house. That's important, that it's *above* the house. Fracking rattling the mountain every which-a-way. These mountains look solid, but they're cracks piled up on cracks. More holes than a sugar junkie's molars. What do you think happens?"

"I have no idea," Mo said, intrigued.

"Old coal mines breathe, just like critters. Sometimes they belch. Especially when somethin' disturbs 'em." His eyes glittered. "Follow me so far?"

"Sure, but he wasn't in the mine, or even near it."

"Oh, but he was close enough. You ever hear of black damp?"

She shook her head.

"Black damp's what a coal mine exhales. CO_2,

nitrogen, maybe a little methane mixed in. Colorless, odorless, and this is the important thing for us, heavier than regular air. Normally it just leaks out in dribs and drabs, but sometimes it collects thick enough that miners who run across it just snuff out like candles." He raised an eyebrow at her.

"So the fracking shakes the coal seam, but if the black damp is heavier than air, how does it get out?"

"Sure has been windy last couple of days, hasn't it? What makes the wind blow?"

And it dawned on her. Excitement filled her as the puzzle finally started to match the picture on the box.

"Change in barometric pressure. Especially a *drop* in pressure."

"Which would?"

"Suck the gas right out of the mine, letting it roll downhill."

Doc Em smiled at her. His satisfaction warmed her own heart.

"And right through the window Jerry opened because it was such a nice day outside."

"So he's sitting at the table doing whatever, the black damp comes through the window, displaces the oxygen. Maybe he has time to feel dizzy, maybe not. Either way, he doesn't have time to get out."

Doc Em finished it off.

"He falls out the chair, maybe dead before he hits the floor. Window's still open, and trailers ain't known for their structural integrity, so by the time the missus shows up, the air inside has normalized again. Death by rapid asphyxia. No marks, no tox, nothing to show why a man who's otherwise healthy as a horse goes down for the count."

They grinned at each other. The poor guy on the slab couldn't appreciate it, but they'd solved this particular death puzzle.

"You write up the report," Doc Em said. "Best you learn the joy of paperwork early on, give you a chance to change your mind about the whole ME thing."

"Not a chance," Mo said, heading for her desk and computer. "I'm sorry for Mrs. Gardner and their family, but this is one I'd never have learned in school."

"One thing you would have learned in time," he said, grin now a little lopsided. "The number one mass murderer in this old world is Mother Nature herself. And she ain't one to discriminate."

He followed her out, dousing the lights behind them.

"You write that report, and I'll call Tom and the funeral home."

He patted her shoulder as he walked by, headed for his own desk.

"Excellent work today, Dr. Fitzgerald. Excellent work."

She smiled.

Felt a little bit of blush, a little bit of pride as she fired up the computer and began typing up the report.

From the desk of Dr. Maureen Fitzgerald, M.E.

KARI KILGORE

AUTHOR OF WICKED BONE AND THE DEFINITION OF CRIME

A Race Against Tea Time

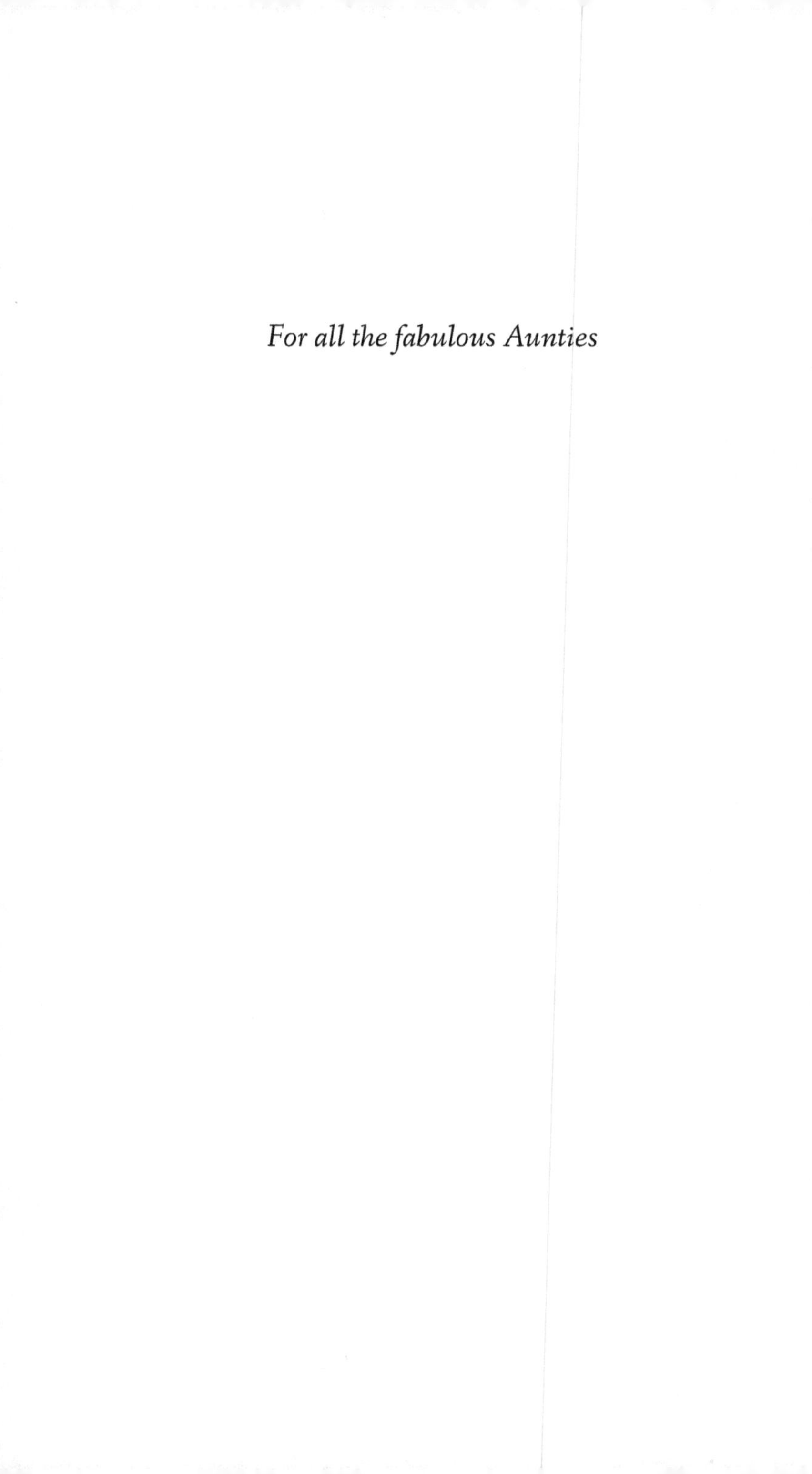

For all the fabulous Aunties

CHAPTER 1

Regina Burke adored the controlled chaos of a rural county courthouse. And the one in Boun County, Virginia, was her favorite by a long shot.

It wasn't anything like what most people imagined, for one thing. The pale gray stone building with grand, white pillars out front was nearly one-hundred-thirty years old, built back when years started with eighteen rather than twenty. Which meant modern amenities like broadband internet, enough electrical outlets, and reliable heating and cooling weren't exactly a given.

Regina doubted her smartphone would get enough signal through the thick walls to function more than a few feet away from the old rippled glass windows. If she'd been allowed to bring it into the courthouse at all.

There were courtrooms, of course, handling more than one kind of trial. General district court full of misdemeanors and traffic troubles, circuit court with heavier felonies and higher-end civil cases, the too-often sad juvenile and domestic relations court—they all operated here.

Unlike the well-lit, spacious versions on most of those legal or police TV shows and movies, the court-rooms themselves were generally cramped. Kind of dark in the corners. Occasionally smelling of mildew when the ancient roof sprang yet another leak.

A huge way those courtrooms differed from the fictional versions was the overall noise and activity levels. In Regina's experience from years of working for a small law office in town, hardly anyone ever shouted or gave dramatic speeches. Most witnesses and defendants were nervous and quiet rather than ranting or yelling.

In fact, the mood in most proceedings was hurry up and wait.

For the judge. For a possible plea bargain. For endless hours while a jury attempted to persuade that one stubborn member.

Not Regina's favorite way to spend a long, long day.

Handing routine filing duties, though, here or in other counties? That was an altogether different proposition. One that often brought the chance to get out and drive through the gorgeous Appalachian Mountains. Beautiful in their delicate spring pastels, vivid green late-summer finery, or spectacular autumn red, orange, and yellow. She even enjoyed trekking through winter gray or brilliant white, as long as the roads didn't ice up.

Regina would volunteer for that duty every day of the week and twice on Wednesday.

Today she wasn't out traversing the twisty mountain roads on the way to a neighboring county seat in Holly Creek, Lightning Gap, or Wolf Branch. Just a quick stroll through her hometown of Bountyfield, past blocks full of buildings carved from the same gray stone as the courthouse.

She hadn't appreciated the intricate carvings and details of that fine stonework until she got out and traveled a good bit. A remarkable number of skilled stonemasons had made the long, treacherous journey across the Atlantic a century ago. They left their marks full of pride in small towns all over their adopted region.

On a day like this fine September morning, Regina didn't even mind humidity so thick she could carve it with a butter knife and fill up a pitcher full of water. That's what made the trees and everything else so rich and lush and beautiful year-round.

But she didn't mind that the Boun County Clerk's Office itself had plenty of air conditioning, either. Keeping people cool on a hot day was a happy side effect of protecting the countless historic documents stored inside.

The clerk's office displayed all that constant, controlled motion she loved as well.

At least three different phones rang at all times, and easily that many simultaneous conversations from unseen people joined in for good measure. Those people walked back and forth in what seemed like random motion rather than any kind of pattern.

A long, nearly chest-high counter dominated the room, with the top made of ancient and well-cared for oak. The odd choice of what looked like paneling from the 1970s lined the front, most of it covered with printed county notices of every age and description.

Standing behind the counter and in front of almost ceiling-high shelves stuffed full of folders and papers, an African-American woman the same age as Regina at forty-eight talked into a heavy tan handset and wrote on a yellow legal pad at the same time. She glanced up and winked at Regina without pausing in either activity.

Pam had been Regina's best friend and favorite gossip partner since their high school days and more changes than Regina would ever admit to. They'd attended each other's birthday parties, weddings, and far too many kid-related events. Through bad hair from perms to straighteners, strange squared-off highlights to mutual flirtations with blonde and red. Too many regrettable clothing choices to bear thinking about.

These days Pam wore her hair natural and cropped close with her silver glinting proud, while Regina kept her brunette tresses touched up and ponytail long. They'd each settled into comfortable business casual wardrobes a good bit more forgiving of their *mature* figures. Regina had shed one husband and happily built a new life with a much better match, while Pam and her perfect-from-the-start partner fussed and quarreled and kissed and snuggled into middle age.

And working together as often as they did was every bit as much fun as they'd always daydreamed back in school.

Pam hung up the phone with a big, coffee-scented sigh and an exaggerated eye roll. Her hands kept writing, tearing the sheet off, and neatly folding it without needing any observation.

"*Please* tell me you have something more interesting than yet another complaint about who has to clean up the buckeye nuts along Walter Franklyn's property line. Every year the same arguments about those blasted trees."

Regina snorted. "I doubt it's interesting, but it should be a whole lot less stressful. Got a couple of filings for Mr. Steffens."

Before Pam could answer, a very young woman came clip-clopping around the edge of the gigantic shelf behind her. Regina would have sworn this child couldn't be more than fourteen years old. Never mind how her towering wedge heels, carefully perfect makeup, and the fact that she was working at the courthouse in the middle of the day suggested she had to be at least a high school graduate.

"Urgent from Sheriff Collier," the youngster said, handing a Pam a pale blue paper. "She needs a list of any retail businesses in Boun County who sell herbal tea. Brewed or take-home."

Pam scowled. "What on earth? Did she say why?"

In that instant, the near-girl transformed herself in front of Pam and Regina's eyes. She glanced left and right, then all her upright, uptight young profes-sional veneer fell away. She leaned in close and spoke in the low voice of someone with a juicy scoop.

"An herbal supplier from just over the border got

arrested this morning. Apparently they got into a dispute with one of their customers, the one who puts together those special blends of Mountain Moonlight Herbal tea. So the supplier mixed jimsonweed instead of valerian into one of them, hoping to frame the tea people for the whole thing."

Pam scowled, still looking confused. But Regina put one hand over her pounding heart.

"Are you saying that tea got sent out?" she said. "When? How did they get that much jimsonweed?"

The young woman nodded. "Shipments are scheduled to arrive today. The problem is trying to get ahead of this before anyone actually drinks the nasty stuff. Apparently they found a big patch at an old mining site. Gathered it up and dried it back in August. The big worry now is figuring out if they slipped the seeds into something else. They're even worse than the leaves."

Regina grabbed at her right pants pocket, where her phone usually was.

Where it *wasn't* inside the courthouse.

"Damn it all to hell. Boun County *could* join the Commonwealth of Virginia in the modern era and allow cell phones in here, but *ohhhh noooo*. Can I use your phone, Pam?"

Now Pam looked as worried as Regina felt. She held up the blue paper.

"I'll get this to Sheriff Collier ASAP. Thanks for the heads-up, Trina." As soon as Trina smiled, put her professional self back on, and clip-clopped away, Pam set the wide, bulky office phone up on the wide oak counter. "Dial nine to get an outside line. What's wrong, Reg?"

Regina pushed the flat buttons with a trembling hand.

"My nephew Trevor. I know you've been to his cute little natural grocery and home delivery shop. One of his biggest sellers is Mountain Moonlight Herbal Tea. He has a wholesale account with them, so he buys for a whole bunch of people and smaller businesses. The most popular tea is their Sound Sleep Tea. With *valerian*. I drink it myself, and I've given it to you and every one of our kids."

Trevor's cheerful voice popped up on the line right away, saying he was sorry he missed the call.

"Voicemail," Regina said, squeezing her eyes closed. "Trev, this is Aunt Reg. Give me a call as soon as you get this, okay? Or call the clerk's office and ask for Pam, or the sheriff's office. You're not in trouble. Well, not really, not now, but that's not... Never mind. Just call me, hon." She hung up the phone. "I've never understood how that kid runs such a successful business when his phone is dead half the time."

"Okay, then we'll send a deputy out, or call one of his customers." Pam was already typing away at a keyboard tucked away out of sight, staring at a monitor hidden below the oak counter. "Want to tell me why this...what did she say...jimsonweed is such a problem?"

"If you'll reach me that phonebook I know you have back there. I don't care that it's twenty years old, the farm supply's number never changes. He takes his big deliveries there. Jimsonweed is poisonous. Trevor told me all about it after some class he took on toxic plants in North America. I remembered it because it grows *every*where."

A printer whirred to life somewhere nearby as Regina flipped through the ancient, smudged yellowish pages, so dry they crackled when she turned them.

"There," Pam said. "Got the list emailed to Sherriff Collier, and a note to ask all the deputies to keep an eye out for Trevor. Printing a copy of everyone else who sells the tea in town in case you need it. You mean this stuff can *kill* people?"

"Not usually, but it happens," Regina said, trying not to grit her teeth as the phone rang and rang over at the farm supply. "It's about as far from valerian as you can get, though. Instead of calming folks down, helping them sleep, jimsonweed makes their hearts race, blood pressure shoot up. If they get enough, they can hallucinate or even get downright violent. Hospitals have to restrain people to treat them sometimes."

Pam reached out to grab Regina's hand with fingers cool from the air conditioning. A man with an old-time mountain accent as thick and slow as winter molasses finally answered the phone.

"Boun County Farm Supply, y'got Tom Wilson here. What can I do for you today?"

"Yes, hi Tom, can you please tell me if Trevor Grigsby has picked up his shipment today? This is his aunt, Regina Hall."

"Sure did, ma'am. Headed out of here 'bout five minutes ago."

Regina shook her head and squeezed Pam's hand. Her speaking way too fast didn't speed up Tom Wilson's deliberate cadence one tiny bit, but she couldn't manage to slow down.

"Did he happen to say where he was going? I tried him on his cell but couldn't get him."

"Well now, he said something about deliveries, I think. Mentioned running a few errands along the way. He was carrying on about all those cats he takes care of chewing up his phone charger again, like I've heard him say before. So I figure he might be runnin' out to get one of those, too."

"Okay. Okay, thank you, Tom. Listen, if you see Trevor, or hear from him, can you ask him to call me? Or the sheriff's office? Or the county clerk's office? It's urgent. Wait, do you know if anyone else gets deliveries of that tea there? The Mountain Moonlight tea? No one should drink it if they do. They're recalling all of it, but especially the Sound Sleep kind. This latest batch isn't...they had a problem with it, and it isn't safe."

"I sure will let you know if I see or hear from him, ma'am, and tell him to call. I can't recall anyone else getting their tea delivered here, no. Most folks get it from stores in town. Or from your young nephew. I'll spread the word as I can about not drinking what came in today. You be sure to let me know if I can do anything else to help."

Regina hung up the phone and rubbed at the spot right between her eyebrows, where most of her tension and all of her impending wrinkles seemed to go.

"He's already gone, out making deliveries or maybe running his usual hundred and one errands he does for everyone he meets. Including to get a new cell phone charger because one of his crazy cats chewed his up, again."

"His cats?" Pam said with a quiver of laughter in her voice. "I understand that being at the root of everything that goes wrong. The little monster darlings we adopted from him would rather gnaw on those little cables and ink pens and everything else than eat." She patted Regina's hand, and Regina finally let out a snort of her own.

Of all the ridiculous and frightening ways to start out a morning.

Pam nodded once and moved the phone back down behind the counter.

"What we're doing to do is call Trevor's store right now," she said. "He always has someone there, right? During the day? They'll give us the list of his delivery customers and help get the word out for folks to watch for him. And not to drink that tea. You'll start calling them, and I'll call anywhere I can think of that sells those cables that might as well be made out of solid gold for what they cost. We'll get him tracked down, Reg."

Regina shook her head. "No, I don't want to disrupt you like that. I'll go back to the office, call from there. We should see about getting it out over the radio station, too, not that anyone outside of town picks that up. Or maybe I should get out and look for him? I know where some of his customers live. But then he might not be able to reach me if he tries. Cell service is rotten once you get too far outside of town even if your phone's not dead."

Pam waved one arm toward the side, where the counter ended with a towering pile of paperwork stacked way too high in a massive inbox. Modern era with email and jump drives and cloud storage or not, rural courthouses still functioned on a never-ending river of paper.

"No, now you're talking nonsense," Pam said. "I expect Art Steffens can do without you for a while, until we catch this wayward nephew of yours. I know I'm not going to be able to concentrate on anything else until we get this sorted out. Neither will you. The deputies know to keep an eye out for him, or they will once I call down to Sherriff Collier's office and make sure they know what's going on. She'll put out an APB for sure. They're already following up with the other places who sell that tea, remember?"

"I know, but I really need to—"

Pam shook her head sharply, once to the left, then the right.

"You really *need* to get around here and start making phone calls. Trevor could run into a whole bunch of trouble over this, his fault or not. I'm guessing the folks he delivers to aren't in the best of health. From what you're telling me about this jimsonweed, we need to make damn sure they don't brew it up thinking they can settle down for their afternoon naps."

Regina held her breath, trying not to imagine Trevor's face if he was part of something like that happening, through no fault of his own, and even with his usual best of intentions.

He'd been a sweet kid from the day he was born, quiet and gentle in her brother's family full of cheerful, boisterous extroverts. When they'd picked up and made a sensible move to Cincinnati for work years ago, Trevor had been heartbroken, staying in constant touch with Regina. She was sure he'd left whirls of dust in his path when he'd moved back to Bountyfield the instant he finished college out in Blacksburg.

She could wish all day long for a drone or a helicopter, or a high-tech satellite tracking device in his adorable little blue delivery van that wouldn't work on narrow mountain roads anyway.

Or, she could do her best to help him like she always had.

"Thank you, Pam. Show me where I won't be in your way. We'll find him."

CHAPTER 2

Trevor fumbled at the phone buzzing in his jeans pocket, hoping to see who was trying to call before the dang thing shut itself down.

Sure enough, the red battery icon flashed on the screen for a second before it went dark.

He stood still on the cracked black asphalt parking lot of the convenience store on the outskirts of town, sweating and wondering if he should go back in and beg their phone for a minute. Not that he had much choice with pay phones a thing of his distant childhood memories.

Maybe someone at his own grocery store would know who was trying to reach him.

He glanced back at the convenience store, plate glass windows covered with huge marketing posters faded from years of hanging in the hot sun. It was true you could buy all manner of beer, soda, snacks, and even assorted auto parts there. Trevor had an ice-cold bottle of soda cooling his hand down right now, that he'd prefer to be cooling down his throat instead.

A few tourist trinkets from the nearby charming mountain towns. The latest attraction being the newly discovered caves just outside of Bountyfield, not far from where he stood.

The one thing he could *not* get, despite all the promises shouted in big bold type, was a cable for his iPhone. They were flat sold out.

Probably to other cat people.

Eh, he had plenty to do today already. No need to add more to the list by calling in.

He turned away and walked toward his goofy looking car/van. Too big to be a car, not big enough for a van, and he refused to add that "a" in the middle as if he had a fleet of vehicles and trailers and wagons following along the twisty roads behind him.

He appreciated his parents for finding it for him, no matter how weird the wedge-shaped front end looked with a huge boxy backside. Plenty of room for cat carriers for his fosters and rescues, piles of cat food and litter, and of course, his shipments and deliveries for everyone else.

All that and an actual CD player too, so he could borrow audiobooks from the library.

Whatever he might have thought when he was a shy, nerdy high school kid, appearances weren't everything after all. His shaggy brown hair and faded Virginia Tech t-shirt pretty much proved that point.

He trusted Brandy back at his store to handle whatever came up. Promoting her to assistant manager a year ago was what let Trevor expand into delivery in the first place. And with the new shipment of tea ready to add to the bags and boxes already packed, delivery was the very thing that needed doing today.

Well, delivery and errands. Like getting a new charging cable.

Because he could swear his three resident cats made sure to teach each new foster cat arrival how to chew right through one before Trevor could manage to say NO. No matter what he sprayed on the cables: lemon, cayenne, or bitter anti-chewing formulas. No matter how well he tried to hide them.

The cats found a way.

He stepped up into the car/van's surprisingly comfortable seat, thankful to get the air conditioning going on such a muggy morning. Maybe he'd finally spring for one of those braided cables, reinforced with metal. See if that kept the shark-cat beasties at bay for a little while.

That meant a drive over toward Holly Creek, or

maybe on to Hidden Springs for bigger stores. It didn't make a whole lot of sense to buy another cheap cable for the cats to devour while he waited for an online shopping delivery.

Besides, in his current delivery boy mode, Trevor was the last one who should be turning to the internet rather than supporting his fellow local businesses.

Decision made, he adjusted his mental map for all the houses, souvenir and trinket shops, and other merchants he could deliver to along the way. His phone wouldn't have gotten signal most of the drive in any case, so it was just as well.

No one was expecting him back before the end of the day anyway.

His time was his own.

Trevor turned up the A/C, hit Play on his latest audiobook CD, and headed out.

CHAPTER 3

Regina sat back in the uncomfortable old rolling office chair, squeezing her eyes closed and rubbing her temples with one hand. She picked up her second cup of lukewarm coffee with the other, deciding the heartburn sure to follow was worth it.

A printed list on the battered and scarred wooden desk in front of her had several phone numbers crossed out at the top. Trevor's customers she'd already contacted in town.

No luck on finding him. But she'd left word for him to call, and to spread the word about today's delivery of herbal tea.

She'd tried his phone several more times too, just in case.

Either in a bad signal zone or the battery was still flat.

She'd never taken part in a mountain gossip relay product recall before. Hopefully it would do the job.

The bottom third of the long list was also crossed out with two big lines. Brandy over at Trevor's store was calling them in between helping walk-in customers. Just like Regina had suspected, Brandy didn't expect to hear a word from him all day. Said he loved getting out and running the roads on delivery days, having time to himself for a change.

Regina opened her eyes to her cramped temporary work area in the clerk's office. Nothing more than a tiny desk wedged into an overstuffed filing room. A lamp, a phone, and one uncomfortable chair. Enough for what she needed right now, though, so she was glad to have it.

And frustrated all the same.

Pam leaned her head around the corner, eyebrows raised and looking hopeful. She had her fabulous red cat-eye reading glasses set with glittering purple stones down low on her nose.

"Hey, finally found a place where he *has* been. That old convenience store on the edge of town, the Stanley's place we used to try to get to sell us beer back when we first started driving. They said he was there probably about fifteen minutes ago, looking for a phone cable."

Regina let out her breath in an upward rush so hard her bangs lifted off her forehead.

"Good! So that means he's headed toward...where? Wolf Branch, maybe?"

Pam shrugged. "Could be. A few roads meet right there, that's how they manage to stay open. He didn't say anything about where he was going to the folks inside. From there he could easily get to Wolf Branch, Laurel Gap, even Hidden Springs. Wouldn't be that far out of the way to head to Lightning Gap or Holly Creek, either."

Regina stared down at the list in front of her, trying not to get annoyed with herself. Starting with locations in Bountyfield made sense at the time. Now she'd just shift over toward...

"I guess I'll start calling along the road to Wolf Branch. Did that APB for his van go out?"

"Sure did, pretty much as soon as you came in here. They got the word out to the radio station too, but you know hardly anyone listens to that these days. Trina said it's out on the county's Facebook and Twitter. I'm not sure that will reach who we're aiming for. You need more coffee, hon?"

"No, thank you, but I might need some antacids if this keeps up for long. I'm hoping some of the people Trevor delivers to might be listening, you know? My in-laws still do. Hardly any of them will be checking social media, but that sure can't hurt."

"We'll keep some people safe, anyway," Pam said. "I just wish we had more than fifteen patrol cars out. That's not much for almost four hundred square miles." She started to leave, then paused. "You okay?"

Regina realized she was staring into space, mainly because her brain had told her body to cease operations.

"You know more about this kind of thing than I do, Pam. Did Sherriff Collier send the APB out to the surrounding counties?"

"I'll make sure of that, or strongly suggest it. Trevor could already be over the county line in pretty much any direction."

"Great, thank you." Regina sat up and picked up her pen again. "This is going to sound strange, but I didn't think we'd be trying to chase down some asshole's poison revenge tea when I woke up this morning either. Do you have any kind of...I don't know, phone tree with the other county clerks?"

"You mean a way to get them on the job with us? I'll see what I can do."

CHAPTER 4

Trevor walked back down the wooden porch steps, glancing back over his shoulder to make absolutely sure he'd re-latched the screen door. He wasn't quite sure what good flipping the curved metal latch down on the outside of an empty house would do, but that didn't matter one bit.

Mrs. Woodrow kept her cozy white clapboard house and porch and yard neat as a pin. She had her own way of doing things that had served her well for every bit of eighty-one years. Anything he messed up along the way *would* be noticed.

Satisfied that he'd left her usual summertime order of tupelo and orange blossom honey, peppermint oil to keep the ants away, and three boxes of Mountain Moonlight Sound Sleep Tea in the right spot and everything was in its right place, he headed back toward his car/van.

This house was so shady and nice he almost wished he could curl up on the porch swing and read an actual print book, or maybe just take a nap. Fond as Mrs. Woodrow and her grandson were of him, he doubted either of them would appreciate finding him there when she got back from her regular doctor's appointment. That was pretty much the only time she left home these days.

Trevor had four more deliveries along this lovely riverside back road before he got back to the main road. May as well keep moving. He was about to get hungry, for one thing.

He'd made great time so far. Eight deliveries to houses and two roadside shops, with someone home (or answering the door) at only three of the houses. Not too much time spent chit-chatting and gossiping everywhere else. Just enough to have a nice conversation and be polite.

But the return trip would feel a lot longer after a long day if he started back after dark.

Right before he got back in the car/van, he heard the bright, chirping ring of a phone inside the house. He'd taken his own useless electronic lump of a phone out of his pocket after his first stop of the day.

No use carrying it around so it could annoy him all day long.

Now it mocked him from the cupholder where he usually put it when he was driving. Within reach of the charging port, which he could be using *if* he hadn't absent-mindedly carried his spare inside more than once. Or taken it in on purpose to replace a chewed one several days ago, and forgotten to pick up more.

Maybe he'd make a quick detour once he got back to the main road.

If he remembered correctly—and he usually did—the little electronics shop in Maple Ridge had a pretty good selection of cables and such. The people who ran the touristy maple barn up there had said to check back in the last time he dropped by, too.

Never hurt to pick up another good customer. And maybe some of that maple candy his Aunt Reg liked so well while he was at it.

CHAPTER 5

Regina carefully placed the handset in the cradle, doing everything she could to keep a strong grip on her temper. No sense in yelling and screaming and swearing in a space she was borrowing for the day, and certainly not in the courthouse of all places.

She rubbed at her left ear, trying to ease the irritation from making more phone calls than she usually did in a week.

She counted to ten, slowly and deliberately.

Then she pounded both fists on the ancient desk several times, letting out a string of white-hot cuss words that she barely managed to keep under her breath.

Pam popped around the corner again, exactly the way Regina hoped she wouldn't. The sparkling glasses now perched on top of her short black and iron gray hair.

"What happened? Did you find him?"

Regina growled low in her throat and flattened her hands on the desk.

"Unfortunately, no. I did not find him. I could have, maybe. If I'd called that house about ten minutes ago. Or maybe it was five. Could be half an hour, or more. And that wasn't anyone's great-grand-parent, either. That was nothing but a punky kid who should have a job and be working as hard as Trevor does. I could hear video games screeching in the background!"

Pam smiled in that oddly upside-down way people used when they were trying to be sympa-thetic. The way that generally worked when Regina wasn't so tense and overstressed.

"That means you know one place he *has* been, right? Does that help you figure out where to call next?"

Regina scrubbed her fingers through hair she'd long since given up on keeping neat. She was certain her makeup was gone, too, and a rather unpleasant aroma of anxiety sweat floated up from her armpits.

An old map of Boun County and the counties nearby—sort of faded and smeared from being photo-copied too many times—had joined the list on the scarred desk. She pointed to several spots she'd circled, some in green, some in red.

"It's like he's jumping around all over the place instead of going in a logical path. That or I'm hitting a whole bunch of houses where he's dropped stuff off but nobody was home. I've gotten several answering machines or phones that just ring and ring. The good news is I've told everyone who did answer not to drink that blasted tea. Or to have him call if he shows up."

"Same here. Between me and Trina, all the other shops who normally sell the stuff know. Several have already returned a bunch of boxes to the post office for the recall. Still no word from the deputies, but they're still on the lookout for him and spreading the word as they can. In all the surrounding counties, too."

Regina lowered her chin to her chest, wincing at the shift in her tense neck and shoulder muscles.

"That *child*," she said in a harsh whisper. "When this is all over I'm going to get him ten of those rein-forced metal charging cables and put half of them in his van myself. I might even sneak a tracking device in there, too. Big shipping companies have those, so I figure a delivery business run by my sweet, maddening nephew can too."

"I'll be happy to contribute to that little project.

Maybe that can be my early Christmas present to him. Very early." Pam walked behind the cramped desk and expertly rubbed Regina's knotted shoulders with her cool hands. "We're all here for you, Aunt Reg. What do you want us to do next?"

Regina touched one of Pam's hand for a second as she slowly raised her head.

"I appreciate all of you more than you know. Trevor will too, when this is all over. Okay. If I play a good old-fashioned game of connect the dots, which means I have to take the chance of ignoring a whole lot of little side roads he could be on, he's more or less on the way to Wolf Branch."

She tapped the map with her pen, on a spot where one of the thin lines Trevor might be following crossed over not one but two thicker lines.

"Unless he detours for Hidden Springs," she said, "Which could also make sense with bigger stores over there. If anything at all made sense today."

"He doesn't have delivery customers that far out, right?"

"Unfortunately, no. Not that are on this list. But you know how he is, Pam. He loves to get out and talk to people. Brandy reminded me he could find ten new customers today and drop off free samples like he usually does. Everyone used to think he was shy when he was a kid, I know I did. Once he got out on his own and away from my brother's rowdy family, Trevor found his confidence. The problem is right now that's part of what's causing all this trouble."

Pam squeezed Regina's shoulders before she stepped away.

"No matter what happens, this isn't his fault. Or yours. He just drove right into a bunch of weird things happening all at once. I don't know a whole lot about the area around Wolf Branch, but I know a few people over that way. I'll see if any of them have ideas of where Trevor might stop and visit."

"That's a good idea," Regina said. "I'll get back to calling. You know what's getting to me? His customers I do talk to—the ones who aren't too damn busy with video games to pay attention, anyway—they're all in a rush to defend him. Telling me he wouldn't ever do anything to hurt them. How they'd do *anything* to help him."

Pam slipped her glasses back down onto her nose.

"He's a good kid, Reg. And you're a good aunt. We'll do everything we can to help, too."

"He is a good kid," Regina whispered to herself after Pam was gone. She circled the name Wolf Branch on her faded map in red. "I don't know if I'm going to hug him or wring his neck first."

She was scared to death someone was going to get really sick because of all of this, or maybe even worse. And worried sick about how awful Trevor would feel either way if someone drank a cup of poisonous jimsonweed tea that he gave them.

"Get somewhere and stay *still* for a few minutes, Trev. Give us a chance to keep this mess from getting worse."

She picked up the phone, holding it to her right ear for a change, and started dialing.

CHAPTER 6

Trevor managed to stop himself from grinning ear to ear until he walked out the broad barn door of the Maple Ridge Maple Barn.

The town itself was absolutely beautiful, perched high up in the mountains, totally surrounded by a ring of massive, gnarled old maple trees. An unusually high number of expensive and varied shops lined the charming main street full of well-maintained brick buildings.

Maple Ridge managed that kind of prosperity way up in the middle of nowhere thanks to those maple trees, and to the carefully antique barnwood design of the maple barn itself. The place was a spectacular display of touristy kitsch, with every cheap souvenir and useless trinket and embarrassingly hillbilly cliché he could imagine.

He'd just been treated to a fascinating tour of the real guts of the place: the syrup processing facilities out back. Where the real magic of the town came from.

The best maple syrup and candy he'd ever tasted, responsible for bringing in a steady stream of tourists and locals alike. Willing and eager to trade their hard-earned cash for that and everything else.

Soon to include his supply of Mountain Moonlight Herbal Tea.

While his store back in Bountyfield would soon be one of the rare handful outside of the Maple Ridge Maple Barn carrying every form of that incredible, addictive maple goodness.

All that, *and* they stocked a line of cell phone cables that were advertised as pet-proof. Trevor wasn't sure about that, not until his toothy monster felines did their worst to prove it wrong. But the cable he plugged into his car/van's outlet and into his poor, depleted phone was just about too stiff to bend.

That had to be a good sign.

He smiled and sighed when the little green battery with a lightning bolt in the middle flashed on the phone's screen. A few minutes to let the battery recover from absolute zero, and he'd be back in business.

He'd just started the engine when he heard a

series of strange chirping noises behind him, followed by an odd blue and red light. He jumped when someone tapped his driver side window.

Then gasped when he saw the brown uniform and gold star of a sheriff's deputy waiting by the door.

Trevor fumbled for the button to roll the window down, annoyed with himself for that instant "What did I do wrong?" reaction that had his heart racing for no good reason. Maybe someday he'd get old enough to outgrow that.

"Hi there," the young woman said. "Trevor Grigsby?"

That didn't calm Trevor's shaking hands one tiny bit.

"Yeah, that's me."

To his relief, the deputy smiled.

"I sure am glad to see you. Deputy Heather Grant, out of Wolf Branch. You're not in trouble, don't worry. But I do have two questions for you."

Trevor managed to swallow and turned off the engine.

"Sure, whatever I can do to help."

Deputy Grant jerked her chin toward the maple barn.

"Did you happen to leave any valerian tea inside?"

That made no sense whatsoever, but Trevor nodded. The deputy waved her arm at another officer. He nodded once and walked inside.

"Okay, we'll get that taken care of. Now, I can see you have your phone plugged in there. Have you checked your messages today?"

Trevor glanced at the phone, then back at the deputy. Now that he didn't seem to be in trouble, he was getting more curious than startled.

"Have I... Well, no. The cat...one of my cats, anyway, chewed right through the cable. I don't usually call in on my delivery day, really. It might be charged enough to start up now. Why, what's wrong? Is anyone hurt?"

She smiled and shook her head.

"I'm happy to say no one's hurt that I know of. A whole lot of people have worked to make sure of that. You have more friends than you think. I'd suggest you give your Aunt Reg a call and let her be the one to explain. We'll wait to see if there's anything we need to help follow up on."

She touched her fingertips to her broad-brimmed hat and walked toward the maple barn.

Trevor stared after her for a second, more confused than ever. Aunt Reg? He'd picked up a bag full of maple candy for her, sure, but he couldn't imagine what she'd need to talk to him about.

When he picked up his phone, his eyes widened and his jaw dropped. Maple Ridge must have a cell tower tucked up here, too, because he had full signal.

Along with *thirty-two* voice messages. He couldn't remember ever getting more than a couple in one day before.

Despite the deputy's reassurances, his heart sped up again while he waited for the call to go through.

"*Trevor!* Thank goodness you called, sweetheart. I think everything is going to be okay, but let's make sure. You're not driving, are you?"

By the time she finished explaining, Trevor was a thousand times grateful he was sitting still.

CHAPTER 7

Chaotic and busy as the courthouse was during the day, it was even more eerie and quiet at night. After the last case had been closed, the last filing recorded, the last fee collected.

Even in the busy hive of the clerk's office, almost all was still.

Rather than the constant buzz of conversation and phones ringing and people walking back and forth, only one low voice spoke, around the corner and out of sight.

Pam, getting an update from the sheriff's department. The last one, with any luck, at least where Operation Retrieve All the Tainted Tea was concerned.

Regina was still in the tiny closet of a file room she'd occupied all day long, but she'd traded out the sit-bone-bruising chair for a more comfortable model. Trevor sat across from her, apparently not minding her previous chair's lack of manners or comfort.

Now that the crisis was nearly contained, she was relieved she'd decided to hug his neck instead of wringing it. The kid was still pale, with the dazed, staring-into-space demeanor of someone who'd gotten a nasty surprise, mixed in with a boatload of exhaustion.

Which was no wonder at all, since he'd retraced every single stop along his delivery route to make absolutely sure everyone was okay.

And to gather up all the recalled tea he could.

He had managed to keep it together long enough to bring over a supply of treats for everyone at the courthouse and the sheriff's department. Assorted cookies Brandy whipped up, along with a collection of every type of candy and chocolate they had on hand.

The candied ginger was Regina's favorite at the moment. A close second behind the maple candy he'd brought from Maple Ridge of all places, where they'd *finally* caught up with him.

The ginger put out the too-much-coffee-and-worry heartburn like a charm.

Trevor shook his head and focused when Pam walked in and just about collapsed into a third chair they'd managed to wedge in. Her wonderful glasses now glittered from the collar of her blouse, where she'd tucked them a good hour ago.

Her eyes looked about as tired—and as relieved—as Regina felt.

"That was Sherriff Collier," Pam said. "They rounded up the last delivery just now, bringing it back here. And, not one of those boxes of Sound Sleep tea had been opened yet. We got to everyone early enough in the day. So you've apologized enough for today, tomorrow, and here on out 'til forever. It's all okay, Trevor. It's all going to be okay."

Regina watched his shoulders slowly rise and fall, and his head sank down much like hers had earlier. When he looked up, his weary eyes were rimmed with red.

"What a nightmare," he said in a shaky voice. "Can you imagine? What could have happened? I mean, I doubt a single one of them will ever trust me again, but it could have been so, so much worse."

Regina resisted the urge to brush back his too-long hair. She didn't have room to talk with the tangled mess on top of her own head. She touched his shoulder instead, and smiled as Pam did the same.

"I don't think so, Trev," Regina said. "Every single one of them knows this wasn't your fault. And that you and people who care about you made sure none of them got hurt. Remember how I told you everyone I talked to kept telling me they'd do anything they could to help you?"

He shrugged and shook his head, but she saw a trace of a smile.

"That's because they know you care about them," she said. "And they care about you. Got it, kid?"

He looked up at her, his head tilted at a cocky, smart-ass angle that made her feel a whole lot better.

"Got it. Thank you both, again. I don't know what I could ever do to repay you."

Pam let out a big, joyful laugh and patted his shoulder a few times.

"I know one thing you can do for me, and for your Aunt Reg here. We're going to get you a whole bunch of those fancy charging cables like you got today. How about you keep some in your van? And keep. Your phone. Charged."

"You got it," he said, grinning. "I promise."

Pam pushed herself to her feet with a grunt.

"The other good news is the investigators don't think the jerks who sent out the jimsonweed tea did anything with the seeds. The state police found a big stash of them, so they probably *meant* to. But everything is locked up safe and sound and ready for trial. You two still up for dinner at my place tonight? Every last one of you, and Brandy, are welcome. I figure we should celebrate getting through this day and staying more or less sane."

Regina looked at Trevor, nodding with her eyebrows raised. He stood and pulled her to her feet and pulled both women into a big hug.

"I wouldn't miss it." He leaned back and winked. "I'll even bring the after-dinner tea."

Pam joined Regina in playfully smacking the back of his head.

And the last sound the courthouse heard that night was laughter.

JASON A. ADAMS

Author of *Malaya* and *Freeing the Spirit*

REUNION AND REDEMPTION

To everyone who becomes who they should be.

CHAPTER 1

Tires squealed as the candy-apple red GTO slid through another curve.

John Barton lazily held the steering wheel, bellowing along with Geddy Lee, who sang about a different sort of car but the exact same sort of drive.

John grinned as he checked for gleaming alloy air cars in his rear-view mirror.

He loved nothing more than driving his '69 monster on twisty mountain roads, and his Appalachian homeland was simply perfect for it.

Wind flew in the open windows, blowing through his blond curls, trying to sneak past his studded leather jacket. The sweet aroma of hot metal combined with the loamy autumn air, filling his senses. The engine roared as it gobbled its way through another gallon of hi-test.

Every nerve was awake. The car spoke to him through the seat, through his hands, and through his feet as he clutched and dropped the heavy four-speed tranny down a gear.

Up ahead, he saw the first few houses and the sign marking the Laurel Gap corporate limits.

John sighed as he eased off the gas pedal. All good things must come to an end, he supposed. Or at least a pause.

Cruising down the main drag, he looked for any changes to the tiny mountain town. And didn't see any. The same Hardees with the same bunch of high-school kids hanging in the parking lot. The vehicles looked a little newer, but they were still pickup trucks. Mullets and rattails turned his way as he cranked Rush up a little louder.

Mullins Hardware, with its bench of old farts spitting brown sludge on the sidewalk. Fannie Meade's Kurl Up and Dye, full of chattering women in to touch up their blue rinse and pass along the latest town gossip. Jamie Patterson's Sunoco station-slash-diner, where you could fill your tank and your belly at the same time.

Depressing.

Hey, the Tastee-Freeze still looked open. Maybe he'd stop by for a peanut butter milkshake, although these days he'd probably get through two sips of the throat-clotting goo. Thick, rich, and sweeter than a first kiss.

Also about a zillion calories and probably loaded with cholesterol. Definitely not the thing for a man looking to keep his skinny jeans.

John pulled up to the window and ordered a large.

A young girl with heavy black mascara and a mouth full of braces behind her smelly strawberry lip gloss traded him five bucks for a huge foam cup that weighed about a pound. John thanked her and drove back down Main Street, giving his cheeks a workout as he struggled to draw a mouthful of his second-favorite childhood treat.

With any luck, he'd bump into his favorite some-time this weekend.

He'd been in Atlanta for ten years, ever since the day after he graduated high school. The ATL stayed in non-stop flux as new buildings went up, old ones came down. He had a family of friends that stayed pretty stable, but the rest of the population came and went.

Different skin colors, different accents, different clothes.

All different. Always changing.

Not at all like dear old Laurel Gap.

Shit, he hadn't had a broken nose in ten whole years.

He passed under a banner welcoming the guests of the Laurel Gap High Ten-Year Reunion. Waste of paint, since most of them probably only had to walk. Still the motel's parking lot was more than half full when he finally pulled in.

"He'p ya?" drawled the grizzled oldtimer behind the counter. Ezra Mullins hadn't changed a bit, along with everything else inside. Still slightly stooped and wearing what looked to be the same dungarees, checked shirt, and red suspenders John had last seen him in.

Ezra—Ezry, in townspeak—was the cousin of Pete Mullins who owned the hardware, and proprietor of the...wait for it...Mullins Motor Lodge. Another of his cousins owned the Mullins IGA grocery, and his brother had Mullins Funeral Home.

Can't spit in Laurel Gap without hitting a Mullins.

John passed over fifty dollars for two nights, took his key, and carried his bag in to the threadbare environs of room 15. He stared at the coarse puke-green upholstery, the bulbous glass lamp which had probably gone from brand new to vintagely retro right there on the beside table, and the twenty-inch RCA TV, complete with rabbit ears.

The ghosts of old farts and bad sex filled the air and he slid the window open as far as it would go and cranked up the air.

It promised to be a long, *long* two days.

CHAPTER 2

Pete Duncan tucked in the shirt of his deputy's uniform and took his pistol belt from the top of the plank dresser as he heard the timid scratching at his door and a soft, mousy voice.

"Breakfast is ready, honey."

Pete turned and walked to his bedroom door in the house they'd lived in since Granny Fleming had died and passed the place down, giving his mom a quick hug before she winced and pulled away.

Pete tried not to wonder about that wince.

He flipped the light switch, sending the bedroom into darkness. No problem, since he knew where the bed and dresser were, and there wasn't much else to trip over. Not unless the huge cross on the wall over his headboard fell off. Hadn't happened so far, not unless something happened when he was too young to remember.

He followed her down the hall, like a bear following Goldilocks. A Goldilocks who wore the same long-sleeved, shapeless gray dress day in and day out.

He'd never understood how she could manage all the chores around their old farmhouse and garden. Unlike Pete's own six-two and two-twenty, his mother might have topped five feet, at least before her back and shoulders got so bowed down by hard work and by...by other things.

She wasn't yet forty-five, but her hair—waist-length when not knotted up in a tight bun most days—was already more gray than red, and her gaunt frame carried no extra flesh.

But she could hoist milk cans from the barn, wrangle the hogs, and knead bread for the whole church without breaking a sweat.

A fine work horse, as his dad liked to comment.

Usually in front of his congregation.

Breakfast smells filled the kitchen as Pete walked in. His mother, as usual, had filled the table with plates piled with fried eggs, stacks of buttered toast, piles of her homemade sausages, and the half-cooked floppy bacon his dad preferred. Pete liked his a bit more crispy and less trichinotic, but what dad liked, dad got.

Jack Duncan sat at the table already, pushing eggs onto his fork with a piece of toast.

"About time, woman," he said giving her a glare from under his heavy black eyebrows. "Fetch me more coffee. You read your Bible lesson this morning, boy?"

"Yes, sir." Another slog through Romans and Corinthians. Pete read those chapters every morning. Had ever since he was four and his dad had caught him in pigtails. The old man had stropped him so black and blue he couldn't sit back in a chair for two weeks.

Pete'd doubled down after high school, trying to purge his sinful desires. He still felt them, but hadn't fallen prey in years.

He sat across from his dad, wondering what sort of mood the old man was in this morning. His dad wasn't quite as big as Pete was, and looked younger than his fifty years. Probably due to lack of any smile lines. While Pete had gotten his mother's carrot top, his dad's hair was short, thick, and black as coal. He kept it plastered flat and parted in the middle, giving him the look of an Alfalfa who drove his friends away.

As his mother turned away from the eggs she was

tending in a huge cast iron skillet, Pete began filling his plate with everything but the bacon. His mother filled his dad's coffee cup, and she asked Pete if he'd like milk or juice.

"Don't treat the boy like a baby, woman. Pour him a cup of coal."

"Dad, you know I don't like—"

Pete shut his mouth when his dad stopped chewing and gave him The Look.

"'Scuse me, boy. What was that?"

"Nothing, sir," Pete muttered.

Crisis averted, his dad went back to shoveling up his food.

"Don't get all in a pout, boy. A *man* drinks coffee with his breakfast, isn't that so? Now mind you say grace."

Pete muttered something he hoped the old man would take as agreement, gave a quick prayer, and used the excuse of eating to avoid any other comment.

Pete and his dad worked their way through breakfast, while his mom shuffled back and forth between stove, coffeepot, and table. How she never bumped into anything was anyone's guess, since she never looked up from the ground.

He hoped she'd eat once he and his dad left for

the day. He assumed she *must* eat, although he'd rarely seen her do so.

"Ezry tells me folks are startin' to show for the big reunion tomorrow," his dad said, finally pushing back from his empty plate and mug.

"Yeah. We've been working on a patrol schedule. Probably going to be a lot—"

"You and the other brownies gonna keep ' em on the straight and narrow? Lock up all the drinkers and what all?"

Pete sighed.

"We're going to keep the peace, Dad. We've got to make—"

"Probably spend the whole weekend in drink. Sinners. That's all they are. Lock ' em all up."

"It's not that simple, Dad. They have to break—"

"There's man's law and there's God's law, boy. Which do you hold higher?"

"I took an oath to—"

"Ezry told me John Barton's stayin' at the motel. Showed up in a fancy car, wearin' fancy clothes."

Pete brightened for the first time. "Really? John's here in town? Man, that's great. I haven't seen him since—"

"You don't want to talk to that...that...whatever he is, boy. Just stay away. Unless you want to arrest him for having the gall to show his face."

"What? Come on, Dad. John's a good—"

"He ain't a good anything, except maybe a good example to folks of how the Devil does."

"I always liked Johnny."

Pete and his dad both turned toward his mother. Pete wasn't sure she'd actually spoken, her voice was always so quiet.

"What was that?" his dad said, his own voice gone quiet. Pete tensed.

"I always thought Johnny was a nice boy," she said, still looking at the floor.

"When I want *your* opinion, woman, I'll give it to you."

CHAPTER 3

J ohn walked down the sidewalk toward Caboose Park, wondering if he had a chance in hell of finding a decent bagel. Probably not, since that was the sort of thing his open-minded Ma liked to call "Jew food."

Some Jew food would be lovely right about now. A bagel covered with schmear and lox, a hot knish with mustard, maybe a...

His stomach finally got distracted when he heard the sound of a car pulling up alongside. A quick flash of blue lights and the blip of a siren.

Oh joy.

Well, it had taken nearly twelve hours, so they must've decided to cut him some slack.

"Halt, John Barton. Place your hands on your head and turn slowly toward the vehicle."

Holy shit, he knew that voice!

Grinning fit to split, John turned and saw Pete Duncan behind the wheel of a deputy's turd-colored cruiser, wearing a matching turd-colored uniform.

Pete was grinning himself, and his smile made John all weak in the knees, and stronger in other places.

"If I resist arrest, officer, will you handcuff me?"

John threw the car in park and jumped out.

"Wow, John. It's good to see you, man. Where you been keeping all these years?"

Pete's red hair was cut even closer than the buzz job he'd had all through school. The big guy had filled out some, pretty impressive since he'd spent four years on the varsity football team. Big shoulders tapered down to narrow hips, and the stripes on his trousers drew John's eyes down, and then back up.

"Oh, you know. Been down in Atlanta, corrupting the young and defiling the old."

Was John imagining it, or was Pete checking him out?

"You look damn good, Pete. I'm glad I...you know..."

And just like that, they were wrapped in a huge hug, slapping each other's back and calling each other foul names.

Finally they broke apart. John's eyes stung, and

Pete looked a bit bloodshot himself. They stood there, staring at each other. John tried to find something witty to say, but came up empty.

All he could seem to manage was more smiles.

"How ya been, Pete? Ever find yourself a good church girl? Get married? Pop out a few rugrats? Or have you decided to go all monkish and celibate?"

Pete's ears reddened. John really, really wanted to touch them, but managed to stay cool. Well...still, anyway.

"Nah, no time for a family. Too busy with my own. I'm still at home, helping out around the place."

"How's your mom? Is she... Is she still okay?" John loved Mrs. Duncan. She'd always treated him good, and never made fun of him or minded his little ways.

"Yeah, she's...you know. Tired. But she still keeps everything up at the house and in the garden." Pete wasn't looking at John now, and the red had moved from his ears to his cheeks.

"I'm sure she does," John said drily. "And how about Jackass? He still kicking you around?"

He immediately regretted the crack when Pete stiffened.

All true, but it wasn't the best way to reintroduce himself.

"Yeah. Dad's still Dad. Still large and in charge."

An uncomfortable silence then. People passed them by and cars trundled back and forth. But for right now, Pete was all there was worth looking at.

The moment passed when Pete shook himself and grinned. "Hey, want to let me give you a tour of the town? Show you all the many, many changes?" He raised an eyebrow and winked at the same time. A neat trick that John wished he could do.

"Why Deputy Pete! I've always *dreamed* I'd someday have an escort in a police uniform. And I won't even have to pay!"

Pete laughed the same old snort-laugh that had always given John the happy tingles, and blushed again, this time all the way from his forehead down under his collar. John desperately wanted to see just how far down that blush went. Hopefully later...

"Just get in the car, funny boy. Hey, want to go grab a bite?"

I'd love to, yes. Where may I bite *you*, Officer Duncan?

Will you bite back?

Please?

Instead of what he wanted to say, John opened the passenger door and slid in.

"Pete, I am in dire need of some good Jew food.

Isn't there *anywhere* in this God-forsaken town that serves a decent bagel?"

"Mr. Barton, I'll need you to shut up now."

CHAPTER 4

P ete and John chatted about this and that as they drove toward The Riverside Diner. Pete was pretty sure they had bagels. At least they might could get something bready with some cream cheese.

John hadn't changed a bit, unless maybe he was more open about himself. They'd first met in grade school, and he'd been Pete's best friend all the way through. He wasn't anything like the people in Pete's family or church.

He'd grown an inch or two since school, and Pete found himself nearly eye to eye with him. Still had the same slender frame, though. Thin but tight, like a dancer. Same curly blond hair, as pretty as a picture. The only real changes were a jaunty slant to his nose and a ruby earring. Pete decided he liked them, and promised himself to get the story about the nose.

But all in all, John was still John.

John was...was *himself*. And that was about the best way to explain him.

Pete had envied him that in school, but had spent the last ten years trying to overcome his own defects and desires.

He prayed all the time. Read his Bible. Studied the lessons.

And stayed single. He knew a good woman would help him purge the Devil, but he hadn't yet met anyone he felt the least bit attracted to.

He was *not* attracted to John. Not anymore.

That was just Satan whispering in his ear.

But that smile. And that voice.

Lord, please show me Thy mercy and save me from myself.

He didn't answer. He never did.

They sat at the diner and ordered what John declared were somewhat passable bagels, at least for freezer case.

"So what made you decide to hit the reunion? The way you skedaddled after graduation, I figured you'd never be back. Thanks for all the phone calls and keeping in touch, by the way."

"Ah, I figured ten years was enough time to risk it," John said. "And besides, I sent you I don't know how many letters after I got settled. I didn't call because...well...your dad might have answered and..."

"I get it. The part about the calls, I mean. But I never got any letter."

John looked at him, hurt in his eyes. Had Pete said something wrong?

"Someday, Peter Duncan, you'll learn to check the mailbox before your old man does."

Had his old man thrown away Pete's mail? He wouldn't have done.

Would he?

John shook himself. Dragged his smile back on.

"Anyway, neither here nor there. Yeah, I'll be at the reunion. Should be fun to see the look on people's faces. How about you?"

Pete shrugged. "I'll be there. In an official capacity. I'm part of the DUI patrol." Which wouldn't be any work, unless someone *too* toasted tried to drive. Ticketing DUIs in town was bad for the local businesses, and the sheriff had told him and the other deputies not to work too hard at it.

"Maybe I can talk you into a walk out behind the vocational building," John said. "You can show me *all* the sights."

Pete looked up and saw John grinning at him. Blood rushed to his face yet again, possibly a new record for blushing. It also rushed farther south as he remembered their last year of school.

The year they'd spent nearly every evening up on the hill behind the VoAg building.

"Come on, John. We're not kids anymore. We can't... *I* can't be doing that...that stuff. You don't still... I mean, you aren't..."

"What, Pete? I'm not what?" John's smile had turned sad. "Not interested? Not attracted to men? Not gay? Is that what you mean?"

"I'm sorry, dude. I didn't—"

"Yes, Pete. Yes, I am. I, John Barton, am gay. Queer as a football bat. Guilty of the sin which dare not speak its name. Happy?"

"Hush!" Pete said, looking quickly around. No one seemed to have heard. "Don't talk like that, man. Not out in public."

"Why not?" John said, raising his voice a little. "I'm not ashamed, Pete. Took getting the fuck away from here and finding some new friends, but I'm happy. *Happy*, Pete. You should try on happy sometime. You might find it suits you."

Just then the waitress came by to check their glasses. John looked away from Pete and up at her.

"Excuse me, ah, Penny," he said, reading her nametag. "I just wanted to tell you that I'm a gay man and I sleep with guys."

"Good for you, sugar," she said, popping her gum as she gave him a confused look. "You end up with a spare, send him my way. This town's dead for decent sex."

John laughed as she walked to the next table.

"See? No one cares. Or at least they *shouldn't* care. Why do you?"

Pete tried, but couldn't make any words come out.

CHAPTER 5

J ohn felt bad for Pete. And for himself, let's be
honest.

Poor Pete. Stuck in that nightmare house
with his nightmare father. Mrs. Duncan was a sweetheart when Jackass wasn't around, but she'd had her
spirit broke long before John met her son.

They left the diner and Pete turned back toward
the cruiser.

"Got your radio and your phone, Deputy?" John
said.

"Well, yeah. Of course."

"Come on then, let's walk back to the park. I've
got a few things I'd like to talk to you about."

Pete hesitated, and John punched him in the
shoulder.

"Oh, come on. It's daylight, you're a cop, and the

park is nice and public. I promise you'll be safe from little old me."

They walked back to the park and leaned against the old red caboose. On a Friday afternoon, they had the place mostly to themselves, except for a few young mothers with strollers who all stayed congregated by the playground over by the restroom shack.

"So what did you want to talk about?" Pete finally asked, not looking at him.

"First of all, you *do* remember all the things we did together, don't you?"

"Yeah, I do." He'd gone quiet, so John had to lean in a little.

"Okay, that's a good start. Ever get yourself a girlfriend?"

"No. No, I..."

"I thought not. Now, instead of asking I'll tell you. I loved you back then, Peter Duncan. I hoped you felt the same way, but I never had the guts to ask." He watched Pete. Waited for his answer.

Pete swallowed, his gaze flicking toward John, then back toward the road.

"I...uh...come on, man. You know I love you like a brother. I just..."

"I don't *want* you to love me like a brother, Pete. I want you to tell me you enjoyed all the things we did as much as I did."

Pete didn't say anything. John felt his temper slipping.

"What is it, huh? Afraid your god might not like you anymore? Or is it your dad that you're afraid of? Afraid he'll love you less, if that's even possible?"

"What we did was a sin, John. Okay, yes. I enjoyed it. But I shouldn't have. The Bible says—"

"The *bible* says 'happy shall he be, that taketh and dasheth thy children against the stones,'" John said, trying to keep himself from shouting. Not very successfully, judging from the way heads turned over by the playground. "Psalm 137. The *bible* says it's cool to rape your drunk dad. The *bible* says it's cool to throw your preteen daughter out to be gang-raped. Why do you want to make that awful book part of your life?"

"But God has His plans, and... He wants..."

John sighed. He needed to calm down and not beat a bible-beater with the bible.

"Look, Pete. You believe in God, right?"

"Yes." Pete's eyes were swimming. John so wanted to take his friend's hands, but he didn't.

"And you believe he loves you and made you and all things just the way they are?"

"Yes."

"So if he made you the way you are, and then told you the way you are is evil and wrong, what then? Would you teach a kid to love dogs, and then torture the kid forever if he petted one?"

"I..."

"Listen, Pete," John said, putting his hand on Pete's shoulder. "If you want to believe in a god, that's your business. But don't let your life be run by what a bunch of ignorant goat herders wrote down three thousand years ago. And don't let your life be run by some evil, wife-beating SOB who only cares about control."

Pete's hands were clenched. He vibrated like a tuning fork as he looked everywhere but at John.

John might have blown it, dammit.

"I need... I can't think about...not right now..."

"I'm sorry, bud," John said, hoping his heart wouldn't shatter. "I don't care about some silly class reunion. I only came back here to find *you*. I guess I should have left you alone."

He would have said more, but right then Pete's cell phone buzzed. He took it from his pocket, looked at the number.

"It's my mother," he said, looking at John with something in his eyes. John wasn't sure what that look meant, exactly.

"Hi, Mom," he said. "No, I'm fine. It's just the pollen. What? Tonight? Yeah, he's right here, I'll ask him." Pete put the phone against his chest.

"Mom wants to know if you'd like to come to dinner."

Dinner at Pete's house.

This should be interesting.

"I'd love to, Mrs. D," he said, talking loud enough for her to hear. "Don't worry," he said more quietly to Pete. "I'll behave, and I'll keep my mouth shut."

CHAPTER 6

Pete picked John up from the hotel that evening. He'd spent the day driving all over the county. There'd been no calls, but he could claim he was on patrol.

He couldn't grab any of the thoughts blowing through his head for very long. Seeing John had brought up all kinds of things he thought he'd dealt with long ago.

Having John sitting right beside him brought up more.

Please, Lord. Please give me guidance and tell me what to do here.

Still no answer.

John didn't say anything as they pulled up to Pete's house. Just sat there staring out the window.

Pete knew he'd hurt John's feelings, somehow. But he had no idea what to do to fix it.

God probably wouldn't help him out with that, either.

They walked up the steps in silence. Went inside in silence. Headed for the kitchen.

When they found his mother, she was sitting in a dining chair.

Back stiff. Hands clutching the arms.

Eyes wide and fixed.

"Hey there, Mrs. D," John said. "Thanks a bunch for inviting…"

She didn't move.

Didn't look at either of them.

Just gripped the chair and stared straight ahead.

"Mom? Are you okay?" Pete knelt beside her, taking her hand. She looked him, gave her head a tiny shake, then looked past his shoulder toward the hall.

Her eyes got wider.

"That you, boy?" Pete's father came in from the other room, rubbing his knuckles with a wet dish-towel. "I see you brought the queerboy. Me and your mother had quite a talk about her invitin' sodomites into my house without permission."

"Dad, don't call John—"

"I tried, boy. I *tried* to raise you right. Beat the

Devil outta you. But you keep right on bringin' him home. I'd thought he might have took the hint on your graduation night. Woman, get your lazy hind end up and fetch my supper." He looked at Pete and John with his smile-free face. "*My* supper. Looks like I'm eatin' alone tonight."

Pete stared at John's face.

At the crooked nose.

His mother got slowly and carefully to her feet, with only the tiniest whimper. She shuffled toward the stove, lit the ring under the iron skillet.

"Dad, did you hit—"

"You need to get on outta my house, queerboy, go back to whatever Gomorrah you been burnin' in for the last ten years. Don't make me teach you again." His father sat at the table. Dropped the dishtowel on the floor.

"Did you hit—"

"I ain't got all night, woman. Where's that food—"

"Dammit, Dad! Did you *hit* my mother?" John stared at his miserable excuse of a father.

The old man just looked back at him, as serenely dour as ever.

"Did you just interrupt me, boy? I know you didn't just."

Pete stared down, his own fists clenched and shaking. His father must have seen something new in Pete's face, because the old man's eyes went from angry to shrewd in a snap, and he put on his favorite mean little smile.

"She musta fell down again. You know how clumsy she gets."

"Jesus, Mrs. D. Do you need me to call somebody?" John moved toward Pete's mother.

"Don't you touch her, queerboy! You get *out* of my house, and I mean right *now!*"

He started to rise, and Pete quickly moved between the old bastard and his friend, but they all stopped when someone else spoke.

"It's my house, Jack."

The three men turned and looked at Pete's mother. She leaned against the counter beside the stove, gripping the edge.

Strain and pain filled her face, but she looked straight at Pete's father.

"What did you say, woman?" he hissed through clenched teeth.

"I said it's *my* house, Jack." Her voice was rising, both in pitch and volume. "*Not* yours! My mother left it to *me*, and *I* say Johnny can stay!"

The old man stood and began rolling up his cuffs.

"Boy, you take your little cocksucker and get the hell out of my house. Me and your mother need to—"

He never finished.

Before Pete could react, his mother snatched the heavy cast iron skillet from the stove, her pain seemingly forgotten as she swung it into the side of his father's head with all her bread-kneading strength.

There was a loud *whang!* Teeth hit the far wall and surprise filled the remaining eye as the old man's head flattened before he hit the floor.

"*MY HOUSE!!*" his mother screamed, bringing the skillet down again and again. "My house, you... you *son of a bitch!* And Johnny can stay! Johnny can stay for supper! And Pete can wear pigtails if he wants! And he doesn't have to drink coffee! And if Johnny and Pete love each other, I'm *glad!* Do you hear me? At least someone in this family will finally know what love *feels* like!"

She brought the skillet down again, and again, and again, not stopping until Pete finally managed to grab her around the waist and pull her against his chest.

John jumped forward and plucked the gory cast iron from her hand.

A jagged crack ran nearly all the way across the black metal.

"Oh, Pete. It's you, honey," she said quietly, looking up at him with a vacant smile. "And Johnny. Hello, dear. Such a nice boy. Would you like to stay and have supper with us?"

Pete and Johnny stared at each other as she went limp and sagged in Pete's arms.

CHAPTER 7

The weekend had come and gone, and neither of them made the reunion after all.

Pete and John sat at the kitchen table. They'd spent the days scrubbing the floor and the walls, grateful for linoleum and Pine-Sol.

"So how did the inquest go?" John asked.

"Quick and simple," Pete said. "Between our testimony and Mom's x-rays, not to mention all the people that came forward and spoke on her behalf, it's a clear case of self-defense, crime of passion, whatever you want to call it. She'll be at the state hospital in Marion, probably for a goodish while, but there won't be any charges."

"I'm sorry, Pete," John said, reaching across the table and touching his hand. "I'm not sorry Jackass is dead, but I'm sorry you're going through all this with your mom and the town and everything."

Pete stood up, went to the window. Stared out at the garden.

"I *knew*, John. I knew all these years. And I never said anything."

"It's not your fault." John had come up beside him. "Shit like this is always a mess, and festers for years. I'm glad your mom finally stood up."

"Me too," Pete whispered.

Would he go to hell for thinking that? Probably not.

He thought maybe there was a reason he never heard any replies to his prayers.

"Look, I don't have to be back in the city for a couple of weeks. I can stay for a while, help you get things sorted out." Pete felt John's hand against his again. He took it, squeezed the fingers.

"I'm sorry too, John. Sorry I never thought to look for your letters. Sorry I..."

"It's okay. I understand."

Pete turned to face him. Saw that something in his eyes that had always been there.

Something that reached down inside Pete to the place that always waited for an answer.

He took both of John's hands in his.

"Can you stay? For a while, anyway? I could use the help and I... I'd like to... I mean..."

"I can stay as long as you'll have me, Officer Duncan," John said, moisture sparkling in his eyes. "And if you want to come visit me, you can stay with me as long as you want."

Pete swallowed. Something huge and lumpy in his throat.

"I want to... I don't know how... Can I..."

"Officer Duncan," John said, with that smile that melted Pete. "I'll need you to shut up now."

And he kissed him.

And just like that, Pete was eighteen again.

But this time he was free, with his whole life in front of him.

Thank you for joining us on this journey through the shadows.
For more from Jason A. Adams and Kari Kilgore, visit www.SpiralPublishing.net or turn the page.

ALSO BY KARI KILGORE

I hope you enjoyed reading the stories in *Shadows Mountain Deep* as much as I enjoyed writing them. You'll find more mystery and crime short stories, novellas, and novels at www.KariKilgore.com/Mystery.

For more adventures from the Appalachian Mountains of Virginia and around the region, and in many genres, head over to www.KariKilgore.com/TalesFromAppalachia.

Check out more of my fiction, including almost every genre, and be first to hear about release dates, Kickstarters and other fun projects, and exclusive e-book and print editions at www.KariKilgore.com.

Novels:

Until Death

The Dream Thief

Hand Me Downs

Protecting Her Own

The Coffee Bomb and the Corporate Spy

The Great Gold Record Heist

Novellas:

Legacy of the Land

In the Pines

DNA Never Lies

The Box of Possibilities

Murder at the Fabulous Feline Emporium

Team Building Revenge

Dispatches from the Galaxy:

Restricted Species

The Becalmed

The Garbage Belt

Plurapod Pathogen

The Changes Cascade

Near Future Forward (with Jason A. Adams)

Dispatches from the Galaxy: A Space Opera Novella Trio

Dangerous Days on a Pleasure Planet

Storms of Future Past:

Dreaming the Storm

Joining the Storm

Into the Storm

Fighting the Storm

Storms of the Heart

Storms of Future Past Omnibus

The Odd Society:

Independent by Means of Magic

Protected by Means of Magic

Voices Through Time:

Songs in the Mountain

Secrets in the Land

Sorrows in the Earth

Walking the Ghosts

Collections:

Fantastic Women: A Dark Fantasy Novella Trio

Fantastic Shorts: Volume 1

Fantastic Shorts: Volume 2

Fantastic Shorts: Volume 3

Escape into Romance: A Collection of Sweet Beginnings

Stepping Out of Reality: Short Spells of Appalachian Magic

Facing Down Extraordinary: A Series of Ordinary Heroes

Hacking Cybercrime: Dana Sanderson Short Mysteries

Investigations Beyond Belief: The Initial Adventures of Deb Powers: Otherworldly PI

Passages in the Real World: Six Stories of Life's Transitions

Fantastic Side Trips: Side Characters Take Center Stage

A Kaleidoscope of Cat Tales: Five Stories of Cats and People Who Love Them

A Tapestry of Holiday Tales: Winter Adventures from the Odds and Endings Bookstore

Aunties Among Us: Five Tales of Fabulous Women

Four-Legged Heroes: When Pets Rescue People

Anthologies with Jason A. Adams:

Partners in Romance

Shadows Mountain Deep: Six Appalachian Crime Tales

Uncommon Holidays: A Different Side of the Season

Partnership in Crime: Six Journeys to Justice

ALSO BY JASON A. ADAMS

I hope you enjoyed reading the stories in *Shadows Mountain Deep* as much as I enjoyed writing them.

Visit www.JasonAdamsBooks.com and join the adventure for exclusive new fiction, my past and future travels, and whatever else strikes my fancy. Hope to see you there!

Novellas:

Agonist

Collections:

Normally Fantastic

On the Case!

Capeless Heroes

Through the Squirrel Tree

Tales From the Squirrel Garden: Volume 1

Anthologies with Kari Kilgore:

Near Future Forward

Partners in Romance

Shadows Mountain Deep

Uncommon Holidays

Partnership in Crime

ABOUT KARI

The daughter, granddaughter, and great-granddaughter of coal miners, Kari Kilgore's wanderlust and imagination lead her all over the world on grand adventures. Her heart and family bring her home to her native Appalachian Mountains of Virginia. From that solid base, she and her husband, fellow author and Appalachian Jason A. Adams, bring those adventures to life in fiction.

Kari is endlessly fascinated by the secrets and mysteries of the mountains around her. And she respects them, too.

Kari writes contemporary fiction, mystery, romance, fantasy, and science fiction, and she's happiest when she surprises herself. She lives with Jason, various house critters, and wildlife they're better off not knowing more about.

The Confidential Adventure Club

For Kari's exclusive free After The End stories and deleted scenes, discounts, early releases, adorable pet photos, Kickstarters and other fun projects, Spiral Publishing Exclusive Edition e-book and print books, and a whole lot more not available anywhere else, join us in The Club.

Hope to see you there!

www.KariKilgore.com
www.SpiralPublishing.net
www.ConfidentialAdventureClub.com

BB bookbub.com/authors/kari-kilgore

a amazon.com/author/karikilgore

g goodreads.com/karikilgore

f facebook.com/kari.kilgore.1

ABOUT JASON

Jason A. Adams writes across the spectrum. His stories include romance, science fiction, fantasy, horror, Appalachian folk tales, and whatever else strikes his fancy.

You can find more of Jason's work and sign up for updates from his Brain Squirrels at www.Jason AdamsBooks.com.

Several more of his stories may be found in *Pulphouse Magazine* and WMG Publishing's Holiday Spectaculars.

A recovering Air Force brat who grew up all over the US and Japan, Jason currently perches in the Appalachian Mountains of Southwest Virginia with his excellent author wife Kari Kilgore (www.KariKilgore.com), various spoiled house critters, and assorted wild visitors from the nearby forest.

News@JasonAdamsBooks.com

ADDITIONAL COPYRIGHT INFORMATION

The Definition of Crime

Discovering the Obvious

www.ingramcontent.com/pod-product-compliance
Lightning Source LLC
Chambersburg PA
CBHW021247200726
48288CB00015B/2577